DRIVING OFF THE MAP

Sharon MacFarlane

DRIVING
OFF THE MAP

SHARON MACFARLANE

Hounslow Press
Toronto · Oxford

Hounslow Press
A Member of the Dundurn Group

Publisher: Anthony Hawke
Editor: Liedewy Hawke
Designer: Sebastian Vasile
Printer: Best Book Manufacturers
Front cover photograph: Sharon MacFarlane

Canadian Cataloguing in Publication Data

MacFarlane, Sharon
    Driving off the map

ISBN 0-88882-192-1

1. Title.

PS8575.F387D74 1997   C813'.54   C96-932587-8
PR9199.3.M33D74 1997

1   2   3   4   5   BJ   01   00   99   98   97

The publisher wishes to acknowledge the generous assistance of the **Saskatchewan Arts Board**, the **Canada Council**, the **Book Publishing Industry Development Program** of the **Department of Canadian Heritage**, and the **Ontario Arts Council**.

Care has been taken to trace the ownership of copyright material used in this book. The author and the publisher welcome any information enabling them to rectify any references or credit in subsequent editions.

Printed and bound in Canada.

Printed on recycled paper. ♲

Hounslow Press
2181 Queen Street East
Suite 301
Toronto, Ontario, Canada
M4E 1E5

Hounslow Press
73 Lime Walk
Headington, Oxford
England
OX3 7AD

Hounslow Press
250 Sonwil Drive
Buffalo, NY
U.S.A. 14225

CONTENTS

For Scotty, Glenda, Fraser, Shannon and Kyra

Acknowledgements

I would like to thank the Saskatchewan Arts Board, the Saskatchewan Writers Guild, and all the friends who encouraged me. I would also like to express my gratitude to Glenda MacFarlane, Liedewy Hawke and Tony Hawke.

Some of the stories in this collection originally appeared in the following:

- *Canadian Forum*: "Winter Dance," "A Short Course in Fitness, Politics, and Interpersonal Relationships."
- *CBC Ambience*: "John and Mac," "A Short Course in Fitness, Politics, and Interpersonal Relationships," "Winter Dance."
- *CBC Arts Wrap*: "Who Are You?"
- *Grain*: "Coffee Row," "Taking It Easy."
- *Herizons*: "We Didn't Go to Len's This Summer."
- *NeWest Review* and *Under NeWest Eyes: Stories from NeWest Review* (NeWest Press): "Stains."
- *Sky High* (Coteau Books), Chapbook (Hag Papers, an imprint of Underwhich Editions): "John and Mac."
- *Zygote*: "Kneading."

Winter Dance

—⊷ ⊷—

Slinging beer was the only job Doug could get after he finally quit boozing. He's on the six o'clock to two AM shift.

The minute he walks into the bar Bud hands him the change apron and disappears to his house behind the hotel. Old Archie, at the table beside the men's can, wakes up and stumbles out the door, leaving a puddle of piss to be mopped up. When Arch dies Bud will have to burn that chair, none of the locals will ever sit in it.

Sam and Lars, at the corner table, are having the same arguments they've had for the last thirty years. Sam wears a green cap with a leaping-deer logo and he claims John Deere is the only kind of machinery worth having on your farm.

Driving off the Map

Lars thinks John Deere is a pile of shit. He wears a Case cap. Lars votes NDP. Sam wouldn't give the time of day to those "Commie bastards"; he supports the Conservatives. Lars swears that Albert Mason cheated the RM out of a thousand dollars in 1961. Sam says it was just a bookkeeping mistake, that Albert is as honest as the day is long.

Stan Ploski and his wife are playing pool. They don't say a word to each other.

Freddy Clark leans on the jukebox, singing along with "The Gambler." He's a little guy and he sings through his nose so he sounds more like Kitty Wells than Kenny Rogers. When the song ends he plays it again.

Just after nine the women come in from the curling rink. They hang their jackets over the backs of their chairs, put their cigarettes and wallets on the table, and arrange their purses carefully on the floor. For some unknown reason Elsie Hartman brings her curling broom into the bar and props it against her chair, where it gets knocked over every time she moves. They don't pool their money or take turns buying rounds — not the women. They pay for their own drinks. "After all, Helen, your gin and tonic costs ten cents more than my Labatt's Lite."

After the first round they start to giggle, after the second Darlene gives Doug shit because there's no Diet Sprite, eating Piggy Puffs the whole time she's bitching about it, and after the third round Mazie starts bawling, she hasn't got any friends in this crappy town and she thinks her husband is screwing around on her and if he is she hasn't got a friend who would put her wise.

Bernie Matheson pushes his coins around on the terry-cloth table cover, trying to make them add up to the price of another vodka. He's come to the end of his welfare check, and the next one's not due for three days. He hardly ever buys groceries now, the money all goes for booze.

Bernie used to be the best ballplayer in the Wild Goose League, a pitcher with a million-dollar arm. He even tried out for the Seattle team one summer. Now he shakes so bad he has to hold his glass in both hands. He's not even forty and the doctor told him he'd be dead in a year if he didn't quit drinking. Poor bugger, Doug thinks, thank Christ I'm not in his shoes.

After the hockey game the fans come in, followed by the players from both teams — all of them dying of thirst. Fifty or sixty people shouting for drinks, chips, cigarettes, popcorn, pizza. Doug's reminded of the time his parents took him to the Saskatoon Exhibition when he was ten. As he walked through the midway all the barkers yelled at him and he put his hands over his ears and ran until he came to a display of machinery in the corner of the fairgrounds and that's where his father found him, sitting in a tractor with the door and windows tightly closed.

But he can't run out now — he's here to sling booze, that's his job. At least tonight there are no fights to break up.

Last call is two AM, but it takes nearly an hour to clear everybody out. One guy always stays behind to tell his life story. Doug figures they draw straws to see whose turn it is. It wouldn't be so bad if the stories were interesting, but they're all the same — the guy's been given a raw deal by his parents or his wife or his boss, sometimes all of them.

When the last glass is washed, the last ashtray emptied, and the puke cleaned up in the washrooms, he switches off the lights and locks the door.

He stands on the sidewalk and takes a deep breath. "Good air in, bad air out." Was that from high-school health class? Maybe he can draw in enough of the cold, clean night to wash the bar crud out of his lungs.

Driving off the Map

His truck stands alone on the street, lightly salted with snow. Using his arm as a broom, he brushes off the windows and hood. He takes a plastic scraper from the sun visor and shaves the frost from the windshield. The engine starts on the third try, but he lets it idle a few minutes before he puts it into gear and drives away.

The thirty-mile drive every night after work is a real pain in the ass. Bud would let him have a room in the hotel, but when his shift is over he wants to get the hell out.

The truck cab is never warm enough. Not in February. Doug shivers in his jeans and thin jacket, switches the heater fan to high and gets lots of noise but no more heat. There are no farms along this strip of gravel road and no other vehicles, not at three o'clock in the morning. He lights a smoke.

He slows for the curve around a big slough. This is the spot where he rolled the Shell fuel truck two years ago last fall. It rolled twice. If it had gone over one more time he'd have been in the water instead of the ditch. He still doesn't know how it happened. He'd downed most of a forty-ouncer that day. He could have been going too fast or maybe he fell asleep, but anyway he wandered over into the thick gravel on the shoulder and flipped.

He remembers waking up. The first thing he saw when he opened his eyes was a white plaster cast on his left leg. Then Suzanne Kutz was standing next to his bed. She had her nurse's cap perched on top of her carroty frizz, so he knew he was in the Palliser hospital.

Then Suzanne was gone and Constable Perrault was there in her place. The interview was short, he remembers that. He was charged with impaired driving.

He got out of the hospital the day before his trial. God, how he hated to walk into that courtroom. The judge fined him six hundred dollars and suspended his license for a year. Of course he got fired. His boss said he'd never be able to trust Doug again. That made Doug feel really crummy because he'd always thought George was his friend.

Worst of all was losing his wife and daughter. Lori said the accident was the last straw. They'd been having lots of arguments in the past year — arguments about money, about her parents, but mostly about his drinking. She kept telling him he was drinking himself to death and he was so sick of hearing it that he told her she was nagging him to death.

Lori took Amanda and went to live in Saskatoon, in a furnished apartment her parents rented for them. Amanda started crying when she realized Doug wasn't coming, and she was still sobbing when the car pulled out of the driveway. Doug went back inside, put his head in his hands and cried too. It all seems like such a long time ago.

He's nearly half-way home now and the truck labours to climb a steep hill. "C'mon, Freckles," Doug says, patting the dashboard. The half-ton was second hand when he bought it. The summer after he finished high school he worked on the road crew and saved up a thousand dollars. The day he drove his truck off the lot he felt like he had the world by the tail. He spent hours washing it and polishing it with Turtle Wax, even took the rubber floor mats into the house and washed them in the bathtub. (His mother wasn't too thrilled about that.) Then he went to Radio Shack and bought the best tape deck they had and installed it himself.

When the first tiny rust spots appeared on the green paint of the fenders and doors Lori named the truck Freckles. Lori had a name for everything. She called their fridge Brett, insisted that's what it said when the motor shut off. The vacuum cleaner was Broomhilda.

Everything's a joke when you're young. When they got married he was nineteen and she was seventeen. The wedding was at the end of June, the day after Lori wrote her last Grade Eleven exam. She said she'd go back to school after the baby was born but she never did. Her parents blamed Doug for that, too. Doug knew they hated his guts — they never made any attempt to hide their feelings. His mom and dad weren't too happy about the marriage either, but at least they hadn't come right out and said it.

They couldn't afford rent for a house so they moved into the suite above the locker plant. They painted all the walls and Doug's grandma gave them a green shag rug for the living room. When all the fancy dishes and ornaments they got for wedding presents were in place, the suite looked real nice. It was great to be together all the time, to make love whenever they wanted. Lori was so pretty then, so sweet.

Amanda was born in November. She had dark hair and blue eyes like Lori, and beautiful long lashes. Doug thought she was perfect. The first time he held her he felt weak with love. He was amazed — he had never suspected he would feel like that.

It was a mutual admiration society. Amanda's eyes lit up whenever she saw him, and when she started to talk the first word she said was "Dad."

He had lots of time to spend with her because his road job ended a month before she was born. They had to make do with his UIC cheques all winter. Even after he started driving the Shell truck for George in April, it seemed like there was never enough money.

Lori's friends in Grade Twelve were going on class trips to Quebec, picking out fancy dresses for grad, and talking about going to university in the fall. She went out and bought a lot of furniture and stuff on credit.

Doug worked at the service station on weekends to make some extra bucks, but it seemed like their debts kept getting bigger instead of smaller. He started dropping into the bar after work. A few beers and bullshitting with his buddies helped him relax and forget his worries for an hour or two.

He stayed in the suite for a few months after Lori and Amanda left, but when he saw that they wouldn't be back no matter how he begged, he moved into an old shack at the east end of town. Lori told him she would never come back until he stopped drinking. When he finally did stop, when he joined AA, it was too late.

She was living with some guy she met at work, she said she didn't want to see Doug any more. She said it was better if he didn't see Amanda either or even phone her.

Hell, maybe she's right, maybe it does confuse kids — having two dads. Amanda goes to kindergarten now. It sure would be great to see her, give her a kiss and a bear hug.

That's the worst thing about this drive every night. There's too much time to think.

He shoves a Jimmy Buffett tape in the deck. The sound is great — the stereo and speakers are worth more than the truck.

He flips the tape back into the box on the seat. Time to garbage these, he thinks, buy some new ones — Michelle Wright or Garth Brooks.

He makes a right turn at the crossroads, starts on the long stretch to Palliser, the last ten miles to home. He passes a deserted farmyard — the house is gone and the barn leans to the east, propped up by a dozen broad planks planted in the ground. A row of overgrown caraganas and a solitary lilac bush have survived fifty years of drought and wind.

A couple of miles farther on he sees something off to the right. The snowy field is bright in the moonlight and there's something waving in the stubble. It looks like little white flags. He slows down to find out what it is and can't believe his eyes. It's a whole bunch of rabbits — jumping straight up into the air. Rabbits. At least a dozen of them.

He stops the truck on the shoulder of the road but keeps the motor running. He slides across the seat, takes his glove and carefully wipes the window on the passenger side. Then he looks out at the field again.

The rabbits are leaping into the air, at least six feet into the air. When one lands, one or two more of them jump; there's a steady stream going up and down. Up and down, with their long white ears pointing straight at the stars.

He's heard about this. Back in Grade Ten, Mr. Sielski, the chemistry teacher, told the class he'd seen what he believed to be a "ritual mating dance of the prairie hare." Then he went into a long-winded description of rabbits doing gymnastics in the field behind his house. Nobody really believed him, after all this was the same guy who swore up and down that the Americans hadn't landed on the moon — it was all fake photography to fool the Russians.

But it's true, it's true. The rabbits are here and they're still dancing — as though a giant popcorn popper is shooting them up into the winter sky. It's absolutely great. He never thought he'd see anything like this. Then he sees something else. Headlights reflect in the rear-view mirror as a car pulls to a stop behind him. A red light ricochets around the cab. Doug knows what's coming next. He rolls down the window and waits.

"Could I see your license and registration, sir?" The mountie's flashlight beam sweeps the cab. When he hands the papers back he asks, "Why are you stopped out here? Are you having trouble?"

"No. No trouble."

The mountie waits, arms akimbo. "Well?"

Doug feels a little grin tugging at the corners of his mouth. "I was watching the rabbits dance."

"Rabbits?" They both look out at the stubble field. Nothing moves; there is no sign of any living creature. Just the stalks of last year's wheat poking through the snow crust. There is a long pause.

"Would you accompany me to the patrol car, sir?"

In the warmth of the cruiser the mountie goes through the required routine: "Do you wish to take this test? If you refuse you can be charged with an offense under the liquor act."

When the mouthpiece is in place, Doug blows. The light is green. "Keep blowing, keep blowing," the mountie persists. The light stays green.

"Have you been drinking tonight, sir?"

"No."

"Where have you been?"

"Denwald. I'm the bartender there."

"And you haven't been drinking?" He sounds skeptical.

"No."

"Then what's this about rabbits?"

"There was a whole lot of them, jumping in the field. Kinda like they were dancing. Haven't you ever heard about them doing that?"

"I'm afraid not. In the province where I was born the rabbits hop, they do not ... dance." He points out the window. "Do you see them now?"

"Nope, they're gone."

The mountie shakes his head and sighs. "All right," he says. "You can go now."

Doug walks back to his truck and the cop calls after him. "And do up your seatbelt."

Driving off the Map

The patrol car follows him all the way to Palliser, slows to a crawl when he pulls into his yard on the outskirts of town, then drives off toward Main Street.

Doug gets out of his truck, leans against the fender and lights a cigarette. He looks across the snow-covered fields and he thinks about the marvel of the little green light and the look on that mountie's face. He thinks about the rabbits — those incredible white puffs leaping into the sky. He's smiling as he walks into the house.

Coffee Row

*P*olly tears the cover off the little cup and pours creamer into her coffee. She twirls the spoon between her fingers for a few moments before she begins stirring.

Palliser stores close on Monday, so most people shop on Tuesdays at the Red & White next door. Then the women (ranging in age from twenty-five to seventy) gather for coffee at the long table in the Bluebird Café. There are eighteen of them today.

The women don't gossip. They leave that to the men, who spend every morning at the Bluebird. What the men don't know, they sometimes invent.

With no planning, a topic always emerges at the women's table. Today it is composting. Sylvie says, "Most food scraps that are put in the garburator could be composted instead."

"Some cities have outlawed garburators," Irene says. "They pollute the water systems."

Ardath laughs. "Yah — and eat silverware."

"Maybe that's what happened to my spoons," Polly says. "My teaspoons have disappeared into thin air. I only have three left. I've got to go to the hardware today and buy more."

"That's odd." Janice pops the soother back into her baby's mouth. "I had to buy more, too — just last week. I'd understand if it was soup spoons; the kids drag them out to the sand pile all summer, but it was just teaspoons."

Tina's frown adds a few more wrinkles to her forehead. "On Sunday when we had the family in for supper, I had to borrow teaspoons from Marie."

Lili comes to the table carrying the glass pot for refills and when she leaves the talk swings back to composters. The group discusses the merits of wooden and plastic bins.

The following Tuesday the topic is amateur drama. The Palliser Players have cancelled their plans to do *The Sound of Music* because they couldn't get enough singers. They are doing *Same Time, Next Year* instead. That only needs two people.

Kate tells about the time she was in a play, and when she was supposed to shoot another actor the sound tape for the gunshot didn't work, so she shouted, "Bang, you're dead!"

Before the laughter has died down, Cheryl says, "My garden fork is gone. It was in the garden shed and the shed is padlocked but the fork is gone." Women push mugs and ashtrays in circles on the plastic tablecloth.

Eileen clears her throat. "So is mine. I left it in the garden patch all summer just like I have for thirty years, but when the forecast was for frost on Saturday I went out to dig the last of the potatoes and it was gone."

Four or five women stand up at once. "Having lunch early today." "Got a doctor's appointment." "Going to the city."

The next Tuesday Polly is the last to arrive. There are several empty chairs at the women's table. The topic is quilting patterns. They discuss the relative difficulty of the Double Wedding Ring and the Cross and the Crown. There are many pauses in the conversation. During one of these they overhear Stan Ploski at the next table.

"Cops asked me five times, 'You say they were self-propelled swathers?' Maybe they figure them swathers drove themselves off the lot. Man, they give me the third degree. I felt like tellin' 'em — if I was tryin' to collect insurance on swathers I woulda picked new ones — not them old pelters I took on trade from Herman."

"Mounties come up with anything yet?" Bob Depoe asks.

"Hell no. It's like them swathers vanished right off the face of the earth."

The women exchange uneasy glances.

"Marilyn is making a bedspread," Kate says. "Log Cabin in pink and burgundy prints."

Polly goes to Kelowna to visit her sister for two weeks, so it is the first Tuesday in November when she gets to coffee row again. Only Cheryl, Eileen, and Tina are there. Hockey is the topic. Everybody has seen the notice in the post office: THERE WILL BE NO PALLISER PIRATES TEAM THIS YEAR.

"What happened?" Polly asks.

"Not enough players — only seven guys." Tina frowns. "Sam says it's the first time that's happened since 1942 when all the guys joined the army."

Driving off the Map

No one speaks. The only sounds in the room are the clink of cups on saucers, the murmur of men's voices, and the hum of the pop cooler.

When Lili appears with the coffee pot, the women all shake their heads. They place their coins in the clean ashtray on the table, pull on their ski jackets, and leave, going their separate ways as soon as they are out the door.

When Polly looks out her bedroom window the next Tuesday, she sees the town is shrouded in thick fog. She has had the 'flu all week and slept the days away — getting up only to have a bath or make a bowl of soup. She is still weak but decides to get dressed and walk to the café. She hasn't seen or talked to anyone since the last coffee row.

Outside it is quiet, as though the fog has smothered sound. Randolph, the cocker spaniel, doesn't bark his usual greeting when Polly passes the MacPhersons. The fog is so thick she can't even tell if he is in the yard.

The 'flu has left Polly feeling light and eggshell-fragile. She walks slowly, placing her feet carefully on the damp sidewalk. Cold penetrates her nylon jacket and fisherman-knit sweater and she shivers. Streetlights cast an eerie glow in the smoke gray fog. Anxious to reach the warmth of the café, Polly quickens her pace. She wonders who will be there and what topic will come up today.

The illuminated Red & White sign appears out of the haze but there are no lights in the window of the store.

That's funny, Polly thinks. She checks her watch. Nine-thirty; it should have been open an hour ago. Even if Marvin and Gladys had slept in, somebody would have phoned them by now. People always run out of milk or bread or something over the weekend — except those who shopped in the city supermarkets on Sunday or Monday.

Polly's glad she doesn't have to walk any further. She pushes the door and steps inside the café. The light inside the pop cooler shows shelves lined with cans of Coke and Pepsi, cartons of juice and chocolate milk. There is no other light in the café. Even the kitchen is dark. Goosebumps form on Polly's arms. "Is anyone here? Lili, where are you?" Silence.

Polly forces herself to walk forward, sliding her outstretched hand on the wall beside her. She finds the panel of switches and clicks them all up. The light that floods the room reveals only empty chairs pulled up to the tables. Polly pushes open the swinging doors to the kitchen. There are no saucepans on the stove, no dishes in the sink, no people.

Polly sits down in her usual chair.

Polly waits.

A Short Course in Fitness, Politics, and Interpersonal Relationships

Sylvie is running. She is running on the Meewasin Valley Trail – the South Saskatchewan River on her left, Saskatoon high-rises on her right. A scene from *Chariots of Fire* flashes on the screen of Sylvie's mind – a slow-motion shot of men, in singlets and shorts, running on a beach. Music swells and ebbs like the ocean in the background.

She imagines herself floating like that, limbs moving in perfect rhythm, long golden hair swept back by the breeze. Sylvie has a good imagination. On this hot August morning she is thirty pounds overweight, her graying hair is short and frizzy, and she runs, not with the grace of an antelope, but with a badger's waddle.

The sun clears the trees and houses on the east side of the river and strikes sparks of light in the water. Sylvie runs under the University Bridge, then looks across the street as she passes the Ukrainian Museum and then the granite walls and spires of Saint John's Anglican Church. In Kiwanis Park the cypress ground cover gives way to beds of ruffled scarlet petunias and white and yellow snapdragons. Sylvie jogs over a little cement bridge, avoiding a large wet spot which sends up ammonia fumes of fresh urine. She follows the curving path between the grass-covered slope and the trees on the riverbank. Traffic sounds are muted, reduced to back-up for birds.

Sweat worms down her forehead. Sweat collects in itchy puddles between her breasts and in the small of her back. Every muscle in her calves is screaming "Stop!" Why not? She could flop down on the grass and go to sleep. Who would know? Who would care? She slows to a plod.

No, damn it, she won't wimp out now. She's run less than a kilometre and she's determined to do at least two. Sylvie has a goal — to run the whole trail, all fifteen kilometres, by Christmas time. She speeds up.

Today is August 16th. The twenty-second day. She started the day after her birthday. The milestone birthday. Andrew and the boys gave her a surprise party but the birthday itself was the biggest surprise. When she saw the

Nifty Fifty banner and candle-covered cake, she suddenly felt old. She'd known she was aging, of course; after all, there were mirrors in the house and her sons were nearly thirty. But she'd never thought about it much until the party. Fifty. She can't even call herself middle-aged any more unless she's sure she could live to be a hundred.

A young woman whizzes past on a bicycle, snatches of rock music seeping from her Walkman. She rides effortlessly, as though her tanned legs could carry her on forever. The woman wears a sleeveless tee-shirt, Spandex shorts, and white runners.

Sylvie wears runners, too — leather Reeboks that cost more than the wedding dress she bought in 1958. The day after her birthday she ate the last piece of cake, drove to the mall and bought shoes at the Foot Locker and a dun-coloured jogging suit in Eaton's Bargain Basement.

Andrew couldn't understand why she wanted to run. His twenty-twenty vision disappeared whenever he looked at her. "So you gained a few pounds," he said. "You still look like a movie star." Yeah, she thought — Roseanne.

She is dieting. She allows herself only salads, fish, and chicken with the skin removed. No red meat, no alcohol, and definitely no ice cream. She is going to lose all the flab. And she is going to get fit. If she doesn't, she'll soon be an old lady with big droopy boobs, a barrel belly, and bulging ankles. She's got to do it and she's got to do it now.

Twenty-two days and it isn't getting one bit easier. She wills herself to go on, thinks about her shower — the reward at the end of the run, a long hot shower, washing away the pain, the sweat, the fatigue. She concentrates on putting one foot in front of the other. Thump, thump, thump, thump — left dusty Reebok, right dusty Reebok, left one again. Got to keep going, got to do it.

Driving off the Map

When she runs past a birch grove the path seems to rise from the ground and settle into place again. Her forearms and fingers are tingling. She sucks in great gulps of air and her chest heaves with the effort. Her lungs are starving. There's not enough air, not enough air in the whole world.

Sylvie is kneeling. She is kneeling on the asphalt path under a poplar tree. She looks up to see arrows of sun slashing down and then sky and leaves pinwheeling coloured fire.

Sylvie is standing. She is standing on the Meewasin Valley Trail — the river behind her, and the Bessborough Hotel in front of her. She is standing at a gate set in the nine-foot-high chain link fence, looking at a sunken garden on the hotel grounds. Seated at a picnic table in the garden is an old man, wearing a gray double-breasted suit and a bright blue tie. The man has bulldog jowls, and his hair springs in silvery waves from a widow's peak. Sylvie sees him there — solid as a wooden table — but she knows he died more than ten years ago. She knows he is buried at the university across the river.

The man rises, comes to the gate, and opens it. "What do you want?" His head jiggles up and down as he speaks.

"Are you ..." she begins, then clears her throat. "You look just like ..." She feels like an idiot. "Are you Mr. Diefenbaker?"

"The Right Honourable John George Diefenbaker." He slips his thumbs under the lapels of his suit jacket and thrusts his chest out. "My fellow Canadian, you see before you the man who won the greatest Conservative victory of the twentieth century."

Sylvie decides not to tell him that Brian Mulroney broke that record in 1984. But she has questions for the Chief. Did you hate John F. Kennedy because of his politics, or because he called you an S.O.B.? What influenced your decision on the Avro Arrow? What's the real scoop on the Munsinger affair? And why did you love Olive more than your first wife? She's gathering the courage to speak, but Diefenbaker has a question of his own.

"Have you seen my driver?"

"Driver?" She looks at the lawn, wonders if there is a mini-golf course somewhere on the grounds. Funny, she thinks, I didn't know he played. Newsmagazines always had pictures of Eisenhower teeing off, but Dief was a fisherman. She remembers a photo of him taken at Waskesieu. He was standing in a canoe, wearing a Siwash sweater and holding a large Northern pike.

"Young fellow, dark hair; his name is John, too."

Sylvie stifles a giggle. He's looking for a chauffeur, not a golf club. "No," she says. "I haven't seen him."

"Can't wait. I'll drive myself." He walks to a black stretch limo parked beside the hotel, his wide pant legs flapping with every step. He gets into the car, slams the door and starts the engine. The window slithers down. "Hurry up, if you're coming."

Sylvie is sitting. She is sitting on the velvet upholstery in the limousine. She buckles her seat belt as Diefenbaker pulls onto Spadina Avenue. A Canadian flag hangs on a pole over the entrance to the Sheraton-Cavalier, the maple leaf bright as blood on the white nylon.

"An abomination," he growls. "Lester Pearson's folly." He's hunched over the wheel, gripping it tightly in liver-spotted hands.

Sylvie's head snaps back as he stomps on the accelerator and whips into the underpass. They are hurtling around the circle like a motorcyclist on the Wall of Death. So he drives like a maniac — fine for him — what's he got to lose? Her left hand grips the seat belt release, her right hand the door handle. Now they're on Spadina North, racing faster and faster. Everything's a blur.

A sharp turn sends them through the parking lot at the Mendel Art Gallery. The car is out of control. They're airborne, flying over the grass, over the red steel fence, over the boat launch. Diefenbaker throws his head back and hoots with laughter. They're gliding. Gliding over the weir, then diving under the CPR Bridge and up again, turning away from the sun.

They climb to a thousand feet and swoop over the airport, doing a loop-the-loop to miss an Air Canada jet that is coming in to land. Sylvie gets a glimpse of the passengers' shocked faces before the car zooms away.

They go over the industrial area, over the Robin Hood mill, the old government elevator and a white-fenced paddock, where three colts gallop in a perfect circle, like horses on a carousel.

They float above the maze of railway tracks on the western outskirts of the city. "Olive and I crossed the country by train in the 1963 campaign. A huge success. And, of course, my last journey was spectacular."

"Your last ... Do you mean the funeral train?"

"All across this country thousands of men, women, and children came to pay their last respects." His tone is reverent. "Many wept. Pageantry unequalled in Canadian history." They observe a few seconds of silence and then he blinks, looks up and says, "I don't know why they moved the CN station way out here. I'll show you where it used to be."

They swing back to the city centre and hover over the Midtown Plaza. "The station was right here. That's where I used to pick up my newspapers — Twenty-first Street and First Avenue — it's called Diefenbaker Corner now. That's where I met Sir Wilfrid Laurier. 1910. I was a fifteen-year-old newsboy. I talked to him for half an hour, but then I told him, 'Well, Mr. Prime Minister, I can't waste any more time. I have to deliver my papers.'" Laughter makes his head jerk up and down like a fiddler's elbow. "Laurier was here to lay the cornerstone at the university, and he talked about me in his speech that day. I'm sure he realized that I was destined for greatness. And, of course, forty-seven years later I was elected prime minister — a position I accepted with the greatest humility."

Humility! This man hasn't had a humble moment since his Grade One teacher gave him an *A* for printing. Sylvie decides to speak up. "I don't need a history lesson, Mr. Diefenbaker."

"Listen here." Dief karate-chops the seat with his left hand. "History is everything. He who does not know the past can never understand the present, and he certainly can do nothing for the future. Remember that, young lady."

Sylvie decides to drop the subject. It's been a very long time since anyone called her "young lady." She looks out at the city spread beneath them — the downtown core dotted with parks, office towers, apartments; the suburbs with their houses nudging fields of ripe grain, and, winding through it all, the blue thread of the South Saskatchewan, tacked in place by seven bridges.

The car is moving again. "Now for the highlight of our tour," Diefenbaker smiles as they swoop over the university campus, skim the roof of the Arts Building, bank sharply over Commerce and Law, and come to a stop thirty feet above the skylight of a handsome building near the riverbank. "The Diefenbaker Centre!" Sylvie hears the fanfare in his voice and suspects she's in for another lecture. The statesman doesn't disappoint her.

"I turned the first sod on September 20, 1975. This building cost three million dollars to construct. The official opening was June 12, 1980. Contains my entire collection of papers, books, and photographs, including my Sir John A. Macdonald material." He's just getting warmed up. "Authentic reconstruction of my East Block Office and Privy Council Chamber, Reading Room, Archives, thousands of invaluable papers, books, video tapes ..."

After five minutes, Sylvie interrupts. "It's closed, you know."

"No, no. It doesn't close until four-thirty."

"You don't understand. It's closed permanently."

"Don't be foolish, woman. The Centre will never close — it will stand forever — a museum, an archival resource, and a monument to my tenure as prime minister of Canada." His eyebrows are drawn together and his eyes are unblinking. He stares at her like an angry owl sizing up a bush rabbit. "There could *never* be a reason for closure."

"They ran out of money to operate it. The university and provincial government cut funds, and Ottawa refused to contribute any more."

"The Liberals must be in power. Just a temporary thing. As soon as my party gets in again, the Centre will be back to normal."

"The Conservatives *are* in. They have been for years."

The old man shakes his head and moans. He seems to have shrunk in on himself. Sylvie wishes she had kept her mouth shut but it's too late now, the damage is done. The limo moves forward a few hundred feet and stops over a simple gravestone set in the grass. The stone bears only the names of John and Olive Diefenbaker, with their birth and death dates. Sylvie is surprised to see that John's date of death is August 16, 1979.

"Yes," he says. "I come back here every year on this date, but that's all over now. All over. The Centre is closed. What a tragedy — the worst thing that's ever happened. Worse even than the nominating convention of 1967." A tear trickles down his wrinkled cheek. "Do you know what I did then, after I was defeated?"

Sylvie shakes her head; she can't bear to look at him.

"I sang. That's right, young lady. I sang." He begins, in a reedy tenor:

When you come to the end of a pur-r-rfect day
He points the car's hood down.
In the firelight's glow
When the lamps burn low
They plummet toward the sunlit river.
And dear friends have to par-r-rt …

Sylvie is lying. She is lying in a bed in Emergency at City Hospital. In the next bed is a woman whose head is turbaned with bandages. She smacks her lips together over toothless gums as though she's sampling a fine wine. An adolescent boy groans in his sleep on the other side. His eyelids fly open; he says, "Pain with a capital P," then goes back to sleep.

Andrew is sitting on a chair beside Sylvie's bed. He smiles at her, but he's cracking his knuckles, so she knows he is worried.

"I drowned," Sylvie says.

"What?" Andrew stops in mid-crack. "No, of course you didn't drown. You fainted."

"Fainted? But the car — the river — we went —"

"The doctor thinks you hyperventilated."

"But how did I get here?"

"We don't really know." He cracks the last knuckle. "It's kind of weird." In the neighbouring bed the wine-taster props herself up on an elbow and pushes the bandage away from her ear.

"Some girl found you behind the Bess, and she ran in and called an ambulance."

"So what's the big mystery?"

"You weren't there when the ambulance arrived."

"Not there? I must have been there."

"The girl said when she went into the hotel there was a guy leaning on a black car, but when she came out he was gone. And so were you."

"But the hospital must know how I got here."

"Emergency was a madhouse; there'd been a bus accident on Thirty-third. Ten or twelve people hurt. But a nurse saw a man carry you in and put you on a bench. He left before she got a chance to talk to him."

"A man? What man?"

"That's what I'd like to know." Andrew's face takes on the "sucking a lemon" expression he gets when he's jealous. "But nobody knows where he went."

Sylvie reaches out and pats her husband's hand. "Tell them to try the Diefenbaker Centre." She yawns and closes her eyes.

Sylvie is walking. She is walking across the parking lot at Westgate Plaza. It is August 17th — twenty-three days since she started running. She lifts the lid of the Salvation Army collection bin and drops a bag inside. The bag contains a dun-coloured jogging suit and a pair of size eight Reeboks.

Sylvie is driving. She is driving to Dairy Queen to order a big, rich, gooey banana split.

Stains

⁓ ⁓

Her wrists burn in the icy water. But the water must be cold if she is to get all the stains out. She folds the leg of the jeans, rubs the layers of heavy denim together. With the bar of harsh laundry soap she scrubs the spots over and over. The water darkens with blood. She twists the jeans, wringing out as much water as she can, sets them carefully beside the sink.

When she lifts the tee-shirt, a small piece of curled, white skin floats free of the jagged tear, rises to the surface. She swallows, takes a deep breath.

When the clothes — a pair of shorts, a pair of socks, the tee-shirt and the jeans — are all in the washer she sits down at the kitchen table. She's never been good at waiting.

"Go home," they told her. "There's nothing you can do here. We'll call you." She stares at the clock, not sure if she wants the hands to move faster or slower. Should she call one of her friends to wait with her? She couldn't bear to make small talk, couldn't concentrate on anything but the pictures that fill her mind. The image of him — gray, unconscious, his dark blood seeping through the bandage, seeping into the white sheet of the hospital bed. No, she will wait now as she waited seventeen years ago for his birth. Alone. She sees again the baby with snowy hair, the five-year-old in an over-sized hockey uniform, the fourth-grade wise man in the school pageant ... thinks of all the hopes she had for him.

She goes to the washer as soon as it stops. There is a circle of red-tinged suds on the inside of the lid. She puts the clothes into the dryer, then with an old towel scrubs the enamel lid. She rinses the towel again and again; when it is clean, she hangs it over the tap to dry.

In the kitchen she fills the kettle and sets it on the burner. She spoons tea leaves into a small brown pot and takes a china mug from the cupboard. When the tea is ready she sits for a moment holding the warm mug in both hands. She drinks two cups but in a few minutes she is thirsty again. Worry parches her mouth; it's always been that way.

She learned to keep a pitcher of water and a glass beside her, the nights she sat up with him when he was sick. With every illness he ran a high fever. When he was a baby and she held him in her arms in the rocking chair all night she wished that she could absorb the heat from his body into her own. Wished him cool — well again — sleeping in his own crib with the white quilt tucked around him. When he was three or four, the fevers made him delirious, made him babble nonsense, reach to pluck imaginary balloons from the air. She thought that when he was older, after he'd had all the childhood diseases, everything would be all right. If only this was as simple as a bout of croup or measles.

The fear has been with her a long time. She realized that when the doorbell rang at 4 AM. She awoke instantly, went to the door, saw the policeman standing there. "... your son — there's been an accident ..." She knew then that, somehow, she'd been waiting for those words.

Noon. He'd be getting up about now if this was an ordinary Saturday. He'd come into the kitchen, bleary-eyed, his hair rumpled, wearing only his wrinkled jeans. He'd go to the fridge, take a drink of milk straight from the carton. She'd say, "For Pete's sake, can't you get a glass?" He'd shrug, both of them knowing she wasn't upset about the milk but about his hangover, his boozing, his friends ... A Saturday ritual that had been going on for a year now. Today there is only the faint hum of the dryer and the ticking of the clock.

When she takes the clothes out of the dryer she spreads them on top of the machine, inspects them carefully, satisfies herself that there is no trace of stains. She folds them and puts them in his dresser. Except the shirt. She takes the shirt to the sewing machine. The gash is so long — from the shoulder almost to the hem — that it distorts the Molson logo printed on the chest. Of course he has other shirts — a red one, a soft silvery gray one, a black one that makes him look even blonder than he is — lots of nice shirts, but he prefers this one. A stretched tee-shirt that shows the world he is a beer-drinker — a man.

In the sewing room she takes a cardboard box from the top shelf. She must find material to match the shirt. She turns the box upside down, spills hundreds of odd-shaped scraps onto the floor. She sifts through them carefully, picks up, then rejects, five or six. Finally she finds a piece of soft cotton that matches exactly the faded blue of the shirt. She pins it carefully in place under the tear and starts sewing. The machine's zigzag stitches pull the edges neatly together. The mend will be almost invisible. But there is still an inch left to sew when the telephone rings.

At the Beachcomber

◥━━◆ ◆━━◤

*I*f she could keep driving Cynthia would be home in half an hour, but an empty gas tank and a full bladder force a stop at the Beachcomber. The Beachcomber, a few miles west of Moose Jaw on Number One Highway, is a gas station/restaurant. Cynthia is returning from a visit to her sister and her family in the Qu'Appelle Valley, and since she is eight months pregnant, she can't go long without a pee break.

Necessities attended to, Cynthia realizes that she is hungry. She drives behind the building and parks her Tercel between a mini-van and a station wagon with B.C. plates. In the restaurant there are only two empty tables, both in the smoking section. She hesitates, thinking she will buy a bag of chips to eat in the car, but when a waitress passes carrying bowls of steaming soup, she decides to sit down. She has eaten the clam chowder here before and she knows it is delicious. Although the Beachcomber is a thousand miles from an ocean, the restaurant specializes in seafood, and the walls are decorated with coloured-glass floats and dusty starfish, captured forever in artistically draped nets. Perhaps the owner is a former Vancouverite or Maritimer or, more likely, he is a prairie chicken who has always dreamed of living by the sea.

Cynthia has a long wait for service. There are only two waitresses and they are almost running in an effort to keep up with orders. She doesn't really mind; she isn't in a hurry and she likes to people-watch. Eavesdropping on strangers in cafés and malls is one of her secret vices. Besides, she is training herself to be more patient. She has acquired a fair amount of patience already, from ten years of teaching kindergarten, but she knows it will be more difficult with a child of her own — a child she and her husband will be responsible for, twenty-four hours a day. She worries that she and Jerry might not be up to the task. What do they know about parenting?

Cynthia takes from her purse the silver spoon her sister, Paula, has made for the baby. She runs her fingers over the smooth bowl and the looped handle, which is engraved with stars and a crescent moon. Cynthia loves going to Paula and Owen's place. Though the house itself is a shabby cabin on the shores of Echo Lake, inside it is vibrant with Owen's paintings and hand-woven throws and rugs. Something intangible makes the rooms cozy and welcoming, and there is a creative energy in the air. The designs Paula uses in her silversmithing spark ideas for Owen's paintings and vice versa. And Matt and Miranda are great, not saints — far from it — but good kids just the same. Miranda has just turned thirteen, and though she is usually in the middle of a pack of giggling girls, she has a serious side. Cynthia has seen some of Miranda's poems, which are witty but show remarkable insight as well. Matt is all arms and legs, a gangly eleven-year-old, who never seems to be in one spot for more than five minutes at a time. When he's not off playing baseball, he's practising his clarinet. Listening to a beginning clarinetist can be a painful experience, since a fingering mistake can send the melody screeching into the upper register with no warning. Owen swore that if he had to hear "Abide with Me" one more time he was going to pitch the clarinet into the lake. Matt just laughed; he knew his dad was really proud of him.

Cynthia had asked Jerry to go with her today, but he stayed home to summerfallow, saying the hot July day was perfect for killing weeds. She was used to his working on Sundays in seeding and harvest but she didn't think it was necessary at this time of year. She grew up in the city but after ten years of teaching in rural communities, she has learned quite a lot about farming. When they were first married, Cynthia had asked Jerry a lot of questions — what crops was he planning to seed, why did he fertilize some fields and not others, why did he prefer Hereford cattle over all other breeds, how did he decide when to start swathing. He always answered in monosyllables. Finally she asked him, point blank, why he seemed to find her questions such a nuisance. Jerry told her that since he farmed in partnership with his brother Walter, and they discussed those topics all day, he found it tiresome to go over everything again with her. Cynthia couldn't understand why he hadn't told her that in the first place; if she hadn't broached the subject he probably would have gone on for the next fifty years giving her answers and resenting the need to do so. Still, she couldn't help feeling hurt that she didn't share in the work that was so important to him.

There was one aspect of farm life, though, that she was only too happy to be excluded from. One day, just over a year ago, she had seen the branding and castrating of the calves. Some farmers made a big occasion of branding, inviting friends and neighbours to help. At the end of the day there was plenty of beer, barbecued hamburgers and, of course, "prairie oysters" — breaded and fried calves' testicles. Cynthia had been to a few of those parties with Jerry, but she had stayed in the house to help with the meal. She had managed to eat one of the "oysters," because she sensed that a refusal would be letting Jerry down in some way.

Jerry and Walter had only a small herd, so they did the job themselves. Curiousity had drawn Cynthia to the barnyard, that June day. She stood beside the barn, where she could observe but wouldn't be in the way. The first thing she saw was the cows, pressed as close to the corral as they could get, their heads butted up against the posts, mouths opened wide in a non-stop chorus of plaintive bawls. The calves, which were no bigger than collie dogs, were running wildly round and round the pen, looking for a way out. From long years of practice, the brothers worked in rhythm, with no wasted motions and no wasted words. Walter reached across the calf's body, his left hand grasping the animal's front leg, his right hand the flank, and with a simultaneous lift and push, flipped the calf's legs out and flopped him on the ground. Then he held the struggling calf in place while Jerry knelt, cut off its testicles, and dropped them in a plastic ice cream bucket. Jerry took a beer bottle and splashed liquid from it onto the cuts. Cynthia caught a faint hint of Lysol smell, which was quickly overpowered by manure. Jerry dropped the bloodied knife on a rock and pulled the branding iron out of the fire. When he pressed the hot iron into the calf's flank, little tongues of flame flared up around it. The animal's bellow of pain and the stench of burning hair were more than Cynthia could bear. She ran away from the barn, into the pasture, stumbling over rocks and clumps of grass until, out of breath, she flopped down on the ground. The scent of wild roses was in the air, and flies buzzed in the wolf willow, but Cynthia smelled only charred hide and heard only the cry of the calf.

She never knew if Jerry had seen her there that day. She never mentioned it and neither did he. She realized, of course, that what he did was a necessary part of raising cattle and that the animals suffered only briefly, but still, sometimes when she watches Jerry at some everyday task — buttering a slice of bread or nailing down a loose shingle — she sees the hot branding iron in those same hands.

After a visit to Paula and Owen's she can't help thinking that she and Jerry really don't share very much. She is excluded from his work, and he wants no part of hers. He knows nothing about teaching and likes it that way. Since they've been married, he's refused to go to her staff parties. He seemed to enjoy them when they were going together, but now he's decided that teachers are a cliquey bunch, who think they're better than everybody else. Cynthia asks herself if she really loves Jerry or if she married him because she was thirty-two years old and she wanted a baby. Did the ticking of the dreaded "biological clock" make her "settle"? No, she loves Jerry, of course she does. He's good to her and hard-working — he'll provide security for their family. It's just that he's so quiet, so reluctant to reveal his feelings, that she's never sure what he is thinking or how he will react to a situation.

"Sorry about the wait." A waitress, with a yachting cap sailing on her permanent wave, appears at Cynthia's elbow. "It's a madhouse in here today."

"No problem. I'll have the clam chowder, an order of brown toast, and a glass of milk."

After the waitress leaves, Cynthia turns her attention to a family group seated to her right. The woman, in her late thirties, has a very pale face framed by straight brown hair. She is oddly dressed for a July day, in a high-necked, long-sleeved blouse and calf-length skirt. The man is a few years older, short and muscular, with neatly trimmed hair and mustache. Between them sits their son, a boy about eleven — Matt's age. While Matt is skinny and wiry, this boy is pudgy, almost obese. His tee-shirt and shorts are two sizes too small. There are dark circles under his eyes.

Because of the noise level in the room, only snatches of their conversation are audible. The mother speaks seldom and so quietly that Cynthia is never able to catch what she is saying.

"Dad, can we go to the Wild Animal Park in Moose Jaw?" the boy asks.

"Why in the name of gawd would you want to stand out in this heat to gape at a bunch of moth-eaten monkeys? They stink to high heaven. The next stop I make is going to be an air-conditioned lounge where I can get a nice cold beer."

Later, the father says, "Water slides? How many times do I have to tell you this trip is costing a bloody fortune. Get it through your pointy little head — I'm not made of money."

Cynthia can't hear the boy's mumbled reply, but the man's face has gone as red as the ketchup on his steak. "Sass me, will you, you little twerp? I've got a damn good notion to leave you at your grandfather's. I'll bet the old man still has the razor strap he used on me; he'll teach you some manners."

When her food arrives Cynthia eats quickly and she is spooning up the last of her soup when the family at the next table leaves. The mother and child go outside while the father strides up to the counter to pay the bill. He waits there, tapping his fingers loudly on the arborite, until one of the waitresses comes to take his money.

Cynthia pays her bill, too, and leaves the restaurant a few minutes later. As she walks around the building, the man is shouting in the parking lot. Although she can't see him, she can hear every word.

"Don't think you can pull that shit with me, young man. I've put up with your whining and bellyaching ever since we left home, but this time you've gone too far. I've had it. Understand?" Silence. A slap. "Now do you understand? Alright, get your sorry ass in the car and I don't want to hear another word out of you 'til at least Winnipeg." Car doors slam and a motor starts up.

Cynthia stands motionless on the pavement, the smell of hot asphalt stinging her nostrils. A station wagon, with an "I Drove the Coquihalla" bumper sticker, comes around the corner, pauses at the stop sign and when there is a break in traffic, pulls into the eastbound lane of the highway. The boy is on his knees in the back seat, staring out the window straight into her eyes.

Cynthia thinks for a minute that she will be sick; she can feel bits of slimy clam rise in her throat. She takes deep breaths and walks to her car, moving as slowly and carefully as a ninety-year-old recovering from a bone fracture. Inside the car, she cranks the air-conditioning to High, adjusting the vents so that the icy stream strikes her face full force.

Driving off the Map

What can she do? It's Sunday, she can't phone Children's Aid. The police? "I want to report that a man slapped his son. No, Officer, I didn't *see* it, but I *heard* it. No, Officer, I don't know who they were or where they were going. But I think they may have come from B.C." Hopeless.

Her baby turns inside her, pushing her abdomen close to the steering wheel. The child is strong and active, getting ready for its birth. In a few short weeks she will be a mother. And Jerry will be a father.

Cynthia backs away from the building and pulls onto the Trans-Canada, heading west, every mile distancing her farther from the boy in the station wagon.

Kneading

What a loser, Wanda thinks, as Del takes his place across from her at the worktable. No surprise — everyone in this class is a loser — all twelve are on Unemployment Insurance. Wanda herself has spent the years since high school in one McJob after another, existing on pogey in between them. Her last job was at the bolt factory and when it shut down six months ago the bureaucrats at UIC insisted she take retraining. Basic Computer Skills sounded like a mind-numbing bore, and she couldn't picture herself hacking up bloody beef carcasses in Meatcutting, so she settled for Commercial Baking.

At least it's warm inside the old bakery where the classes are held, which is just as well, considering it's minus twenty outside and a sixty-kilometre-an-hour wind is lashing dirty snow past the windows.

Del has just come in from the storm. It is a smoke-free building and Del's a two-pack-a-day man, so every time there's a break he pulls on his parka and boogies out to sit in his rusty half-ton to suck back a couple of Export As. It's the only time he comes to life; in class he slouches in his chair and doesn't even bother to take notes. Smoking's probably the reason he's so skinny. Or maybe he doesn't eat enough, can't afford food after he buys ciggies. Maybe that's why he's in Baking; he's hoping to fill up on cakes and pies. His skin hasn't got much more colour than the white tee-shirt and apron he wears. He's even too lazy to grow hair; only a few strands straggle out from under his paper cap, and his mustache is pathetic. His glasses are five years out of style, but behind them his eyes are the rich brown of chocolate-glazed doughnuts. Wanda guesses that he is about her age — pushing thirty.

Today, after all the classroom instruction about the formation of gluten and the chemistry of yeast, they are finally going to learn how to make bread. Old Parkins tells them that although they will be using mechanical mixers when they are employed in bakeries, he is going to show them how to knead by hand so they will get a feel for the process. On the floured table in front of each student he plops a small lump of soggy dough.

Wanda begins to knead, trying to copy the instructor's actions, but the dough sticks between her fingers and won't go where she wants it to; it seems to have a mind of its own. Her efforts to wrestle it into submission are turning the blob a sickly gray colour. She's beginning to think she picked the wrong class — at least in Meatcutting they give you a honking big saw to slash out a rump roast.

She gives the lump a few more desultory slaps, then turns her attention to Del, who is working just a few inches away from her, across the table. His hands move in a sure rhythm, lifting the far side of the dough, folding toward himself, then with the heels of his hands pushing it gently away. A quarter turn of the dough, lift, fold, push. Turn, lift, fold, push. Turn, lift, fold, push. Del has beautiful hands. His fingers are long and slender with clean nails; even the nicotine stains on the index and middle fingers of his right hand look well scrubbed.

Wanda abandons her own dough. The instructor is at the other end of the room, fielding Mrs. Takamoto's endless questions. Mrs. T is a recent widow who hasn't made a decision in thirty years. Wanda is mesmerized by Del's hands; they are strong but gentle at the same time. As he works the white dough, it becomes smoother and shinier. Turn, lift, fold, push. Turn, lift, fold, push. The air is heavy with the aroma of flour and yeast mixed with warm soapy skin and a pinch of cigarette smoke. Wanda pulls off her cardigan and with a crumpled kleenex blots the sweat on her forehead.

Under Del's hands the satiny dough becomes springy and elastic. Wanda imagines his hands on her breasts, the long slender fingers stroking, caressing. She steps right up to the table, pressing as close as she can. The fire that's spreading through her body has nothing to do with the big ovens in the room. Del shapes the dough into a ball, gives it a final pat, and looks up to meet Wanda's eyes. She can sense that the bread is beginning to rise. But the chemistry of yeast is a minor phenomenon compared to what's happening between them.

"Coffee break, fifteen minutes," old Parkins calls as he heads for his office, pulling the door closed just before Mrs. Takamoto catches up to him.

Driving off the Map

Hand in hand Del and Wanda race outside. They don't stop to put on their parkas. He doesn't even take his cigarettes. The storm swirls around Del's ancient Dodge, but there's no need for them to turn on the heater. They kiss as Del unzips her jeans with one hand and performs a bra release with the other. His hands move in dextrous rhythm; they feel exactly the way she had imagined them. Retraining is the smartest thing Wanda's ever done. Who would have thought she'd find a man like Del in a baking class? And who knows? Maybe a year from now they'll be working, the two of them making bread together, alone in the early morning hours, in a steamy bakery somewhere.

Workshop

Day One

*I*t's called a get-acquainted party. Claire is not getting acquainted. She sits in an alcove beside the fireplace and sips red wine from a plastic glass. Whenever someone looks her way she smiles, then shifts her gaze across the room as though she's spotted a friend trying to get her attention. It's a technique she used when she went to her first dance at the age of thirteen – a technique she's had thirty years to perfect.

"Persona." "Did you try M & S?" "Stream of consciousness." "Verisimilitude."

She hasn't got a clue what these people are talking about. And they all seem to know one another already. What on earth is she doing here? Whatever possessed her to sign up for a week-long writers' workshop?

It's clear to her now that winning a prize from the *Palliser Post* for a children's story doesn't make her a real writer.

She could pack up and leave right away. But she dreads the long drive through the hills from this ski resort to Saskatoon and then another two hours on the road to Palliser. She dreads even more the thought of explaining to her family and friends the reason she came home.

She's left casseroles in the freezer and detailed instructions for Gordon and the boys about meals and using the washer and dryer. It's the first time she has ever gone off anywhere on her own. She's worried that something will happen to Blair and Blaine while she is away. Ever since they were babies she's had to fight against her tendency to be overprotective — a "smother mother." They are teenagers now but she still can't bear to see them hurt — whether it's a sprained ankle or a party they aren't invited to. Her place is at home with her family, not in a writing class.

Maybe she should transfer from the Introduction to Fiction class to Researching and Writing Local History. But her town's history book, *Pathways to Palliser*, was published two years ago. Claire smiles. *Pathways* probably belongs in the fiction category, too. Some of its citizens were unrecognizable in the family stories. Snoose Lundgren, the town drunk, was transformed into a community leader in his granddaughter's write-up. Claire doesn't want to write history, though; she wants to write short stories.

The workshop coordinator, a tall bearded man, taps a glass (a real one) for silence. He introduces the instructors. Cynthia, the poetry instructor, is a vivacious redhead who has had three books published. She wears a red jumpsuit, and huge scarlet and silver earrings swing from her pierced ears.

David Henley, the Advanced Fiction teacher, has recently won the Governor-General's Award. He wears a tweed jacket over tee-shirt and jeans.

When he is introduced, the man who is to teach the history class rubs his hand over his hairless scalp and then lights a pipe full of vile tobacco. His name is Wendell and he comes from Edmonton.

Jane Hurst is the "Introduction" teacher. She is about forty-eight, a small woman with soft brown eyes and a warm smile. Her first book will be published in the spring.

When the party ends, Claire goes to her room and reads a short story in an anthology she borrowed from the library. The characters are real people and the story is moving without being sentimental. She knows she will never write anything half as good, no matter how many classes she takes.

She turns out the light, but she can't sleep. She lies flat on her back in the single bed with her hands crossed over her chest like a corpse. She longs to be home in her own bed with the rhythm of Gordon's snores lulling her to sleep. Why did she ever think she wanted to write. Why wasn't she content to just take care of her husband and sons as she'd done for the last twenty years. They appreciated her — praised her cooking and homemade bread.

Why wasn't that enough. Trying to be a writer at the age of forty-three — it was idiotic. She wasn't smart enough; that was obvious. She was the only person in that lounge tonight who hadn't been to university. If she had any sense at all she would have ended her writing career with the publication of "The Magic Treehouse" in the *Palliser Post*.

Day Two

Claire is awake at five-thirty the next morning. She would like a shower but she's afraid the noise will wake the others in the dorm. She gets dressed and stands looking out the window at the dull gray sky and leafless trees. She has always hated fall; it seems such a useless time of year – the growing is all over, with nothing but winter to look forward to.

A young man in a neon tracksuit runs on the path that circles the complex. He has very broad shoulders. She thinks of Blaine, who is as tall as this man, but at fifteen hasn't filled out yet. Claire remembers the jogger is in the Advanced class.

After breakfast the coordinator gives Claire a stack of paper – Xeroxed copies of the items to be workshopped. The first one is a TV script; it looks slick and professional. Next is the first chapter of a novel. A novel? She thought this was a class for beginners. Then a poem which she doesn't understand. She turns the page and sees "Olaf's Pipe," the piece she submitted.

She reads the first paragraph and it's as bad as she feared – a silly story about a contest to choose a town's ugliest man. The boy sitting next to her is reading it too and drawing a highlighter across the page. Claire hopes he doesn't know she is the one who wrote it.

The last item is a funny story about a woman who hates working in her vegetable garden. Claire tries to guess who wrote it. She hates weeding, too. She still helps with haying and harvest but Claire no longer plants an acre of potatoes every spring. After they have finished reading, the instructor stands up and asks, "May we start with yours, Claire?"

Claire says, "Sure, I'll be glad to get it over with." Then she remembers the grammar rule – never end a sentence with a preposition.

Jane explains her workshop method: each person criticizes your story and you can't talk until they are finished. Who could talk with a mouth this dry anyway?

Judith, the scriptwriter, begins. She wears a black beret, a long black dress, no makeup, and a frown. Claire knows she is going to chop her story into a hundred tiny pieces. Judith says, "I liked it." She pauses. "A lot." She points out three grammatical errors. Claire corrects them immediately in her copy. The others all find something they like in the story. Claire can't believe it. Maybe it's so bad they can't think of any way to fix it, so they pretend it's good.

They discuss the TV script and the poem, but Claire is still in a daze. When it's her turn to comment she says something — she isn't sure what — and when the class ends she almost floats out of the room.

Day Three

Cheryl, the woman who has the room next to Claire's, is a young nurse from Saskatoon who has recently married a farmer. Her in-laws — hard-working Mennonites — insisted that she grow a huge garden. At least she got a funny story out of the experience. Cheryl and Claire go to breakfast together.

In class they discuss the chapter of the novel. They all (including the instructor) think it is a Harlequin romance.

"No, it's supposed to be a literary work," the woman who wrote it says in a voice just above a whisper. She looks like she's going to cry. Claire feels really shitty and she's sure the others do too.

Jane asks the class which writers they admire and when Claire says "Anne Tyler," Jane offers to lend her the newest Tyler to read.

There is a line-up for the pay phone when Claire goes to call home after supper. While they wait, the young people talk about Lester, an old man in the history class. Lester looks a bit like Winston Churchill and he snores through the teacher's lectures, then wakes up and tells the class all about the Rumely tractor his father bought in 1931.

Day Four

In the morning Claire writes a new story about a graduation dance. It's fluff. Why can't she write something serious? Something good?

Claire and Cheryl eat lunch with Heather, who is in the Advanced class. Heather has a faint lisp which should be annoying but is somehow pleasant. She is a born story-teller. Heather tells them that the jogger's name is Evan and he is writing a novel about hockey players. His characters are all very macho and treat their women like dirt. She says it will sell very well.

In the evening everyone walks to the town hall for Jane's reading. She has only read a page or two when Lester gets up and goes down the hall to the bathroom. He slams the door and the sound of flushing water competes with Jane's reading. She smiles and carries on.

It's over too soon for Claire. She wants to know how the story ends. When Jane is alone for a moment Claire goes up to her and says, "You write like Margaret Atwood." Jane looks surprised, takes a sip of coffee from the styrofoam cup and says, "Thank you." Claire hopes Jane won't think she is trying to suck up.

Day Five

Evan is lifting weights on the lawn. Today he wears a blue jogging suit.

Claire knows the names of all her neighbours in the dorm now. The young ones run in and out of each other's rooms borrowing computer paper or reading their latest poems. They say "Hi" to Claire when they meet her in the hall. One of them tells her about Lester falling asleep in class and shouting, "Whoa, Dobbin!" so loud he woke himself up.

Workshop goes well. Everyone has some constructive things to say.

It's David Henley's night at the town hall. Lester walks in late and slams the door behind him. David looks up, says, "Hello, Lester," and continues reading his story about Bessie, a tough old broad who beats a young guy at snooker. David says he's been looking for Bessie for years.

Day Six

The class workshops a poem by the tall, gangly boy who sits next to Claire. It's the first thing he's ever written and Claire thinks it's good.

In the evening Claire overhears people making plans to go to the pub, a wind-up because it's the last night. She goes to her room and workshops all the material for the next morning's session. She tries to revise her own story but finds she's reading the same paragraph over and over. She can't come up with one new idea.

Cheryl knocks on her door and calls out, "Enough work. Come on, let's go to the pub."

The writers have pushed three tables together. Cheryl grabs two chairs from an empty table and they squeeze in. The others are laughing, telling jokes. They have been drinking for an hour. Cheryl drinks only ginger ale, but Claire orders a Cæsar. Evan, the jogger, is talking to Cheryl, but Claire doesn't join in the conversation. They are carrying on a mild flirtation and don't need her input.

Using her wallflower technique, she nods and smiles. She drinks two more Cæsars.

Traci, one of the girls in the Poetry class, arm-wrestles with Evan. He pins her arm to the table in two seconds and she has fits of giggles. Cheryl is next, fluttering her eyelashes at Evan as they clasp hands. Her arm hits the terrycloth even faster than Traci's did. More giggles as Evan grins and lifts his hands over his head in a victory gesture.

"Try me." Claire is surprised to hear the words come out of her mouth. Evan shrugs, then turns to her and leans his right elbow on the table. They lock hands and begin. Claire channels all her strength into her right arm. Her head and chest are tight and hot. She can feel the cords in her neck strain. Evan's biceps bulge under the thin cotton of his tee-shirt. Their arms tremble but don't budge. Stalemate. All conversation stops as people crowd in close to watch. Claire is barely aware of them as she concentrates on one final superhuman effort. She can't let him beat her. The muscles in her forearm are on fire. Evan's arm begins to waver and she forces it to the table with the last of her strength.

A cheer goes up, and David Henley shouts, "At last I've found Bessie!" Everyone laughs. Evan's expression changes from surprise to anger. It's the look Claire has seen on her sons' faces when things didn't go their way. For a moment she feels sorry that she has humiliated Evan. But only for a moment.

Claire turns to the other writers who are waiting to talk to her.

Sunday Afternoon

— ❦ —

*F*ive more miles and Ardath will be home. She drives slowly; she's in no hurry to arrive because Sunday afternoon and evening stretch before her. It's hard to believe that Sundays only have twenty-four hours; they seem twice as long as other days.

Today Ardath has been to church for the first time since her husband died. When she opened the door of Palliser United and looked at the front of the room, she saw not the plain wooden pulpit but a gray casket flanked by wreaths of spring flowers. Waves of grief sapped her strength and she sank into the nearest pew, her body so heavy she felt she would never be able to get up.

But after a few moments the casket image disappeared and she began to find comfort in the creamy plaster walls, the felt God Is Love banner, the feel of hymnal pages, the smell of furniture polish and ancient dust, and the sermon delivered in Reverend McKay's familiar monotone. She stayed afterward for coffee and cake in the church basement and visited with her friends in the congregation. In the first weeks after Robert's death she had been invited to someone's house for supper every Sunday, but in time people got on with their own lives and forgot about her. She didn't blame them; she had done the same when her friends were widowed. But she has enjoyed herself today and decides to go to church every week again.

Church without Robert — another first to add to her list: first summer, first birthday (her fifty-ninth) spent alone, and the first crop harvested by custom combiners. But there are many more to come — the first winter and with it the first Christmas, New Year's Eve, and on February 10th, their wedding anniversary. That one will be tough, but she is sure now that she will be able to cope.

It will be easier when her mind stops playing tricks on her. When she no longer begins to read him an interesting item in the newspaper, when she can discover a funny new show on television without thinking *Robert will like this.* Surely, soon she will wake in the morning and remember immediately that Robert's gone; she'll stop imagining that he's in the kitchen brewing coffee.

If only she'd insisted that they sell out when Robert had the first attack, the one the doctor called a warning. But he wanted to keep farming one more year, until his sixty-fifth birthday, because he figured that his pension added to the money from the sale of their land would give them security. He planned to take Ardath to Scotland, his birthplace, and he wanted to have enough money for a grand trip when he took her "home." Still, if she'd insisted he might have sold. He'd be here with her now, not in the Palliser cemetery. If only, if only ... she thought, as she had every day since May 14th.

Ardath knew that Robert had always wanted the best for her. It was his acts of kindness she remembered, not their infrequent arguments when he had wounded her with sarcastic putdowns. She'll have to watch it or she might become like Doreen Pankratz. During their forty years of marriage Doreen's husband had been a lazy, philandering drunk but since his death she had transformed Joe into a model husband and father — a pillar of the community. If the Joe Pankratz of Doreen's memory was resurrected on the main street of Palliser, not a single citizen would recognize him.

The sky, the fields, and the gravel road before Ardath are drained of colour on this sunless cold October day. Fall is a "party's over, nothing to look forward to" season. In spite of the cold and icy roads she even prefers winter because once the fields are covered with snow, gray skies disappear in a wash of delicate blue and the sun shines again.

Ardath turns from the grid road onto her own lane. Her house lies at the end of two miles of this narrow track which climbs and dips over low hills. When she crests the last hill half a mile from home she sees a vehicle stopped in the middle of the road below her. The long dark brown car doesn't belong to any of her neighbours. There isn't room to get by on either side, so she comes to a stop a few feet behind the car, which she can see now is a Lincoln Continental. She can't see a driver. After waiting a few minutes she gets out, buttons her coat, and walks slowly to the other car.

When she is beside the driver's door she looks inside and sees a man slumped forward, his head resting on the steering wheel. Ardath is afraid but she takes a deep breath and taps lightly on the window. The man doesn't move. My God, he's dead, she thinks. A heart attack, just like Robert. Robert lying on the ground while seed wheat poured into the discer, overflowed the boxes, spilled onto the ground, covered Robert's lifeless body. Ardath steps back from the stranger's car.

Don't panic, she tells herself, maybe he's just sleeping. She can see a briefcase and papers piled up on the back seat. Probably a salesman on a long trip — just pulled off the road for a rest. But way out here and on a Sunday? Maybe she should go for help, get one of the neighbours. The nearest farm is Mattson's, three miles away. And how can she get out? She can't turn around, the ditches are too steep. She'll have to drive in reverse all the way to the grid road. No, she can't do that — too far. She'll walk to her house and phone Mattson's. But they won't be home, as soon as harvest is finished they go away every weekend.

She taps on the car window again. No response. She has to do something; she forces herself to open the door. The man is in his early forties and weighs at least three hundred pounds. He wears no jacket, only a short-sleeved shirt and thin dress pants, and when Ardath looks down she sees bare ankles spilling over the sides of his leather shoes. The skin is mottled purple from the cold.

"Hello, are you okay?" No answer. She reaches out and touches his shoulder. "Are you okay?" He stirs, shifts slightly in his seat. Thank God he's alive. "Who are you? What are you doing here?"

He groans, lifts his head and finally focuses his red-rimmed eyes on her.

"Wha, wha?" The grunts are propelled through the chill air on brandy fumes so powerful they are almost visible.

"Who are you?" Ardath asks.

He moves his hands as though he's clawing his way out of a giant cobweb.

"Lea me lone."

"Where are you going?"

He puts his hands on the wheel and pushes himself to an upright position. "Goin' to Mun and Da. Lea me lone."

He must be really lost, Ardath thinks. If his parents lived anywhere in the municipality she would know who he is.

"You can't stay here." Ardath summons up her courage. "You have to move. You're blocking my road."

His response is immediate. "Na your road!" He pounds the steering wheel and shouts, "My fuckin' road."

Ardath is terrified but determined not to show it. She hears herself saying, "Look, I don't know who you are or where you're going but you can't stay here." Her voice sounds almost normal. "If you don't move I'll have to call the police."

His face contorts with fury. "No fuckin' plice." With a swiftness she wouldn't have believed possible he twists the ignition key, yanks the gear lever to Drive and slams his foot on the accelerator. As the car jerks past Ardath, the open door misses her by inches, then swings shut as he drives away. She watches the Lincoln pull into her yard, swing around on her lawn, then head south at great speed across the frozen summerfallow field.

Ardath is shaking as she drives her own car up to the house a few minutes later. Inside she runs to the picture window in the living room, but she can see no sign of the other car. He could be miles away by now. It's impossible to tell which direction he went when he reached the grid road.

She can't think what to do. She can't let him drive around the country — drunk as he is, he'll kill somebody. She goes to the kitchen, takes the phone book from its hook and looks up the number of the RCMP detachment at Denwald. It's hard to dial because her hands are still shaking. After the third ring a recording comes on: "Our office is closed. Please call the Swift Current detachment. Thank you."

Hopeless. She's eighty miles from Swift Current, by the time the police get here, he'll be long gone. She phones Mattson's. No answer. She tries Thompson's, the only other house on the way to town. No answer.

Do something. But what? Don't just sit there. Take action. You're responsible. What about him? He's the one who got drunk and got behind the wheel. But he'd still be safely passed out on your road if you'd left him alone. Now he's out there driving that powerful machine at eighty miles an hour, meeting other cars, and he's so drunk he can't see straight. Round and round her thoughts circle with no conclusion reached, no decision taken.

At last Ardath gets up and locks both the front and back doors. She can't remember ever locking the doors; she doesn't even know where the keys are, she's never needed them before.

Again she considers phoning the police but she knows it's much too late now. If Robert were here, he'd know what to do. And if she had known what to do last year, Robert might be here.

She picks up her library book but reads the same paragraph over three times without taking in the meaning. She turns on TV. Fresh-faced youngsters open their mouths wide to harmonize about sin on *Hymn Sing,* and on the only other channel she can get, race cars whizz round and round a track, accompanied by a buzz-saw whine of engines. She clicks the set off and goes to the phone. She dials Mattson's number – no answer. Thompson's – no answer.

Once again she returns to the window, sees only the lifeless fields waiting for snow. She pictures the stranger somewhere just out of sight, sleeping it off, imagines him waking up sober, driving home carefully.

At four o'clock she makes herself a cup of tea. She wanders from room to room, returning always to the picture window until darkness obscures everything outside the circle of her yard light. She goes to the phone and starts to dial Mattson's, then replaces the receiver. What would I tell them now? Stay off the highways, I sent a dangerous drunk out there.

She turns on TV again but she can't concentrate long enough to figure out the plot of the movie. By this time he might be home, she thinks, sitting with his family watching the very same show. Maybe he's sitting alone in the dark. Or maybe he's hunched over the wheel of that big car hurtling down the yellow line toward a pair of oncoming headlights.

Ardath realizes she is shivering. She turns up the thermostat and goes into the bedroom, leaving the lights on in every room. She puts on her flannelette nightgown and crawls into bed under two blankets and a duvet. She leaves the bedside lamp on high.

Sleep is intermittent and filled with swirling images of long brown cars, God Is Love banners, steep ditches, and overflowing discer boxes. Every hour on the hour she wakes, certain each time that Robert has called her name. But the house is silent except for the whoosh of the furnace.

At 6 AM she turns on the radio beside the bed. "... hurricane off the coast of the Philippines has been downgraded to a tropical storm. In local news, RCMP report that one man was killed last night in a single-vehicle accident thirty kilometers south of Palliser. Identification is being

withheld pending notification of next-of-kin. Now in weather...
a low pressure system ..."

It's him of course – her stranger. She knows she will
remember forever the vulnerable look of those plum-coloured
ankles. And even with her eyes closed tight Ardath can feel
Robert staring at her from the photo on the dresser.

We Didn't Go to Len's This Summer

---

*T*he wife went to a summer school for three weeks, took an art class. I still don't know why she went. Edna's been painting for years and has done some real nice things. We've got two pictures hanging in the living room that she did of our girls, Judy and Karen. The girls both work in Calgary now but Edna copied from their old school photos. And her flower pictures are just beautiful, they've got one she did of a vase of lilacs hanging in the library in town. She took an art correspondence course last winter and I thought that would have been enough, but no, she sent off the money she'd saved up from the egg cheques and enrolled in this summer class. Turned our whole summer upside down, too.

The first two weeks in July, between spraying and summerfallowing, we always go to my brother Len's cabin at Candle Lake. Haven't missed a summer in over twenty years. Len and I like to fish and I always come home with a big bag of jackfish fillets for the deepfreeze. It's a great beach for kids, too — our two and Len's boys used to have a great time there when they were small. Edna and Len's wife, Hazel, made a lot of good meals on that wood stove. Never a cross word between them all those years.

Well, anyway, when Edna came home and I went to meet her bus at Swift Current, I was way too early. Had to sit for an hour in that depot with a lot of dirty hippies. When the bus did get in, she was the last one off. She came down the steps, smiling and waving at me. She looked good, younger somehow. She was wearing a purple dress of some thin material, like cheesecloth. I was sure I'd never seen that before. She gave me a hug right there with everybody watching and said, "It was wonderful," before I even had a chance to say a word. We got her luggage — two suitcases and a big package wrapped in brown paper and tied with heavy twine.

She talked all the way home, telling me about her teachers, her classmates, and what she'd learned. She didn't seem worried when I told her the crops were really suffering, needed rain bad. Then I told her there was a letter from the girls but she said, "Oh, I phoned them when I was at school, we had a nice long talk."

After we got home and had coffee, I pulled her onto my lap and kissed her. She had been gone a long time. She jumped up and I thought she was going to the bedroom, but she took the butcher knife from the rack on the wall and slit the twine on the big package. Edna took out paintings and propped them up against the kitchen cupboards. There must have been a dozen pictures. "Well, what do you think?" she said.

I couldn't believe it. They were all ugly. No flowers, no sunsets, no kittens. The biggest picture was black and red stripes on a green background, some were splotches of all different colours, one was brown and white shapes which might have been horses, but I don't know for sure. The only thing I recognized was a picture of a rubber boot and some cattails. Who in their right mind wants a picture of a rubber boot? What could I say? Edna was waiting. "Nice," I said. Then we went to bed.

The next day Edna moved all her painting stuff into the girls' room, just put their stuffed toys and class pictures and everything into a cardboard box in the corner. She went in there every morning after breakfast and painted until it was time to make lunch. She hardly spent any time working in the garden; I'd never seen it so full of weeds. And we ran out of bread, had to buy some at the store. Awful stuff, tasteless as blotting paper.

Three days after she came home, we finally got rain. It had been cloudy all day and just after supper it started, warm and gentle. Edna went out and stood in the front yard and let the rain wash over her. God knows, no one was happier to see rain than me, but I couldn't see the sense in getting soaking wet when there was no need. When I called her to come in, she just lifted her head and let the water pour down her face.

One day the next week I was summerfallowing on the home quarter so at three o'clock I came in for coffee. I saw a strange car parked in the yard but I thought it was probably a salesman, there had been a lot of them around since the rain had perked the crops up. When I was hanging up my cap in the back porch, Edna opened up the door and said, "Come in and meet one of my classmates from summer school." Her cheeks were flushed.

Sitting at the kitchen table was a guy with long hair and a scraggly beard. He wasn't any older than our Judy, I'm sure. "Glad to meet you, Mr. Phillips," he said, and shook my hand. Then Edna asked if I would like some wine. I saw that they were both drinking white wine from the fancy crystal glasses Edna's grandmother had left her. I had coffee. This Chet told me his dad farmed near Moose Jaw, but when I asked him if they'd had hail in that big storm that went through that way, he didn't even know. Then him and Edna started talking about "composition" and "negative space" and a lot of other rubbish. I put on my cap and went back to the tractor. When I came in at six o'clock he was gone and supper was ready.

Harvest was early and we had a pretty fair crop, even if the rain had come a little too late. Edna hauled grain, like she's always done. We finished harvesting by the first of October. It was sunny and warm, a good fall. I said, "You know — we could meet Len and Hazel up at the cabin on Thanksgiving weekend and still get in some fishing." Do you know what Edna said?

"Why don't you go alone? I'm working on a series of watercolours that I want to finish."

"Hell, Edna," I said. "You can do watercolours any time. Now let's phone Len and tell him we'll be up."

"Tell him *you'll* be up," Edna said. Nothing I said made a bit of difference to that woman; she wouldn't go. I didn't go alone. How would I have explained that to Len and Hazel? So we stayed home. Edna painted and I built a new bin for seed grain. You know, somehow I don't think we'll be going to Len's next summer either.

Looking in the Rearview Mirror

━━✦ ✦━━

*I*n the curved glass of the rearview mirror the narrow road is sucked back to the horizon. Half an hour ago a car of which Ardath hadn't been aware had passed her with a loud blat of its horn. She had been daydreaming, a mistake when she needed all her concentration for the task of driving on the left.

Maybe she shouldn't be driving here. Other sixty-year-old women travel by bus when they visit foreign countries. But Ardath wants to explore at her own pace, go wherever she pleases. Still, the passing car had startled her, so now she checks the mirror frequently.

Driving off the Map

On both sides of the road there are mossy green fields bordered by low stone dykes. Highland cattle turn to stare at her car. With their short curved horns, shaggy auburn hair, and forelocks hanging over their eyes, they are caricatures of cows. They seem friendly, harmless, scaled down like so much in this country.

In many ways, Scotland is what Ardath expected — ruined castles, twisting rivers, and green hills dotted with sheep. She has read the travel books and seen countless photos. And, after all, she was married to a Scot for thirty-seven years.

She thought she was prepared for the rain; she expected a soft mist. She got mist all right, and every other type of rain as well. If the Innuit have a hundred words for snow, the Scots should have at least as many words for rain. When she landed at Glasgow Airport the downpour was so heavy she imagined angry giants hurling buckets of water at the earth. On the train to Aberdeen her windowseat afforded her dreamlike glimpses of countryside and villages beyond the shimmering rain curtain. She had begun to think it would rain forever.

But she awoke to clear skies this morning in Aberchirder. She had spent the night in Robert's hometown, the town he always called Foggieloan, or Foggie. Ardath was surprised and puzzled the first time she received a letter from Robert's mother and saw the Aberchirder postmark. She never did learn how the town got its nickname — only that it meant "grassy field."

She had left her bed-and-breakfast room to explore the three streets that made up the village and then walked past Kinairdy Castle to the ancient cemetery on the banks of the Deveron River.

For nearly an hour she wandered among the stones which were dark with moss and age and seemed to grow out of the earth as naturally as the grass and trees. The Grants were buried at Aberchirder, as their ancestors had been for centuries. At last she found the graves of Robert's parents and his sisters.

She had wondered once more if Robert had wanted to be buried beside them instead of in a Saskatchewan graveyard on a hill that was too steep to farm. Ardath had visited his grave a week ago, the day before her flight. A hundred questions went through her mind as she stood there in the hot July wind, but there were no answers, only the whirr of grasshoppers in the prairie wool.

Once, after they had been to a funeral, she had asked Robert where he wanted to be buried.

"Doesn't matter to me. I'll be dead."

A typical reply. Just another in the long list of things her husband refused to talk about. Now it is too late. She will never know where he wanted to be buried, just as she will never know if he was happy with the choices he made — staying in Saskatchewan, becoming a farmer, marrying her.

Robert had stopped her questions that day so many years ago by taking her in his arms. They often made love after they came home from a funeral. Ardath was never sure if the act was an affirmation of life or if it was being in the house in the middle of the afternoon, dressed in their best clothes, that sparked their desire for each other.

Her husband looked very handsome when he was dressed up. Robert was a big man with rugged features and unruly dark hair, who should have been more at home in his work clothes — jeans and flannel shirts — but when he put on a suit he looked as though he wore one every day of his life.

A lorry looms in the rearview mirror and overtakes with inches to spare. She's amazed at how fast the locals drive on these roads — roads so narrow and full of curves that she can almost believe the story that they were originally paths made by drunken shepherds following crippled sheep. The sun has warmed the car so much that she rolls down the window, admitting air that is so soft it is like a caress on her cheek. Gulls swoop down to the furrows of a newly ploughed field. She is nearing the ocean.

Ardath plans to drive as far as Inverness, turn her rented car in there, and take the train back to Glasgow. For the hundredth time she wishes Robert was beside her. This is the trip they had been planning and saving for for years. Her husband had immigrated to Canada when he was twenty and had never been back to Scotland — not even when his parents died. Robert decided to wait until he was sixty-five so that his pension could give them extra spending money, because he wanted to give her the best possible holiday.

But Robert hadn't lived long enough to collect his pension. A year ago, at seeding time, he died of a heart attack as he was filling the discer boxes with wheat.

There was no green carpet, no sheltering oaks in the cemetery the May afternoon of Robert's funeral, but as the minister spoke the familiar "Ashes to ashes, dust to dust," the clear, liquid notes of a meadowlark's song rose into the prairie sky.

Traffic is heavier now; Ardath's car is in the middle of a long procession of vehicles. A roadside marker says Portsoy 2 Miles. She decides to stop for lunch at this village, which hugs the shore of the North Atlantic.

She parks her car in the town square. It is enclosed by clean, well-kept buildings. Some of the shops are white stucco, but most are stone with small white-framed windows. Beside the door of the Boyne Hotel there is a wooden cutout of a chef with the words Full Meals neatly lettered on his apron.

The dining-room is dim; it is below street level, but there are lit candles in silver candlesticks on the starched cloths at each table. Service is quiet and efficient, and Ardath's cock-a-leekie soup arrives in a delicate china bowl.

A young couple, dressed in sweatshirts and shorts, are the only other customers. Grungy backpacks lie on the floor at their feet. Every few minutes the man leans forward and nuzzles the woman's neck. From overheard snatches of their conversation Ardath can tell they are English.

She is reminded of a cartoon Robert had shown her years ago in one of his *Scots* magazines. It was a drawing of two sailors – one English, the other Scottish. The English sailor had a tattoo on his chest – a big heart with the words I Love Mary inside. The Scottish sailor also had a tattoo of a heart, but the words on his chest were Miss P. Hogg Is Not Too Bad. Robert adopted those words as a code phrase. When another man might have said, "Darling, you're beautiful," or "I adore you," her husband would smile at her and say "Miss P. Hogg is not too bad."

The memory is bittersweet. In all their years together Robert had never put into words the way he felt about her. Now she shifts in her chair so that the lovers are no longer in her line of vision.

After lunch Ardath walks down to the harbour, which is horseshoe-shaped and surrounded on three sides by hills. To her right are tiers of gray apartments and on the left, the ruins of a stone building. Pleasure boats are moored inside the breakwater, but there are none moving on the ocean. She had expected to see fishing trawlers here but there is no sign of them. All her life Ardath has read about the salt tang of the sea but to her it smells like a mixture of tar, wet sand, and fish scales. She sits on a bench for an hour, mesmerized by the dark water and the ruffle of white breaking endlessly on the rocks.

Driving off the Map

Stirred from her lethargy by the arrival of a busload of American tourists, Ardath leaves the bench and crosses to a narrow street on the north arm of the harbour. She is drawn to a two-storey stone building. China cups patterned with thistles and heather are displayed on a length of tartan in the window, so it's obviously a shop but Ardath can't see any signs. She opens a door and enters a cramped room. Shelves and tables are piled with Fair Isle pullovers, linen tea towels printed with recipes for oatcakes and cloutie dumplings, clan maps, kilt pins and cairngorm brooches — all the usual souvenir items. But in a dark corner she finds a locked glass case mounted on the wall. Inside the case are three shelves and on each shelf, six eggs. Each egg stands on a gold filigree ring, which is about half an inch high and an inch and a half in diameter. The eggs appear to be made of polished rock, and although they differ in colour, they are all the same size and shape of a hen's Grade A Large. A small hand-lettered sign taped to the frame of the cabinet says Eggs - £20 Each. Forty dollars. Too much. If she were going to spend that much she would be better off with something practical — one of those wool sweaters.

But her eye keeps going back to an egg on the middle shelf — the one with the striated earth tones: tan, gray, ochre, umber, and brown. But forty dollars for a useless ornament? No, the idea is ridiculous. She begins to thread her way to the door but then she stops and turns to the woman seated on the stool behind the cash register.

"I'd like to buy one of your eggs."

The shopkeeper puts down her romance novel and searches in three drawers before she finds a key to unlock the glass case.

"Which ane do ye fancy?" She swings the door open, removes the egg of Ardath's choice and says, "Will ye be needing the holder? That's another pound."

Ardath hesitates, then realizes she will have no way to display the egg without it. "Yes," she says, seeing in her mind's eye how it will look in her china cabinet at home. After Ardath pays, the shopkeeper hands her the tissue-paper-wrapped egg and holder. The small package is surprisingly heavy.

The sun is shining as she climbs back up the steep hill. At the top she stops to catch her breath and for the first time since she left Canada she sheds her bulky cardigan. Four boys about eight years old are playing soccer on the cobblestones. Three of them are carrot-tops but one lad, taller than the others, has a mop of black hair. She thinks of a photo of Robert taken when he was about ten. It shows a solemn face with an almost frightened expression. He wears a school uniform — white shirt, striped tie, vee-necked pullover, and short pants. The boys in the square wear tee-shirts patterned with the latest Hollywood cartoon characters.

From Portsoy, Ardath drives west along the coastline, passing through the seaside towns of Cullen and Buckie. On impulse she turns left onto a road which takes her into the Spey Valley. There is a roadside map tracing the Whisky Trail — thirty distilleries which produce the Scotch the natives call "uisge beatha" — water of life. The scenery here could have been lifted straight from the cover of a *Visit the Beautiful Highlands* brochure.

A few miles down the road Ardath stops at a lay-by to take a picture of the sun-spangled Spey River. She walks around until she finds a spot where a tall spruce is lined up on each side of her viewfinder. She's taken only a half dozen pictures on her whole trip, this will be her one artistic shot. Robert was the photographer in the family. There are hundreds of photos of her in the albums at home but just a few of her husband.

Driving off the Map

She catches herself just as she is about to unlock the passenger door, glances around to see if anyone is watching, then hurries around to the driver's side. Every time she leaves the car she forgets that steering wheels are on the right-hand side in British vehicles.

Ardath sets her camera down on the car seat and picks up the package she bought in Portsoy. She carefully pulls the paper away and lifts the smooth object in her hand. The egg radiates warmth, as though the earth tones have drawn the sun's rays into its core. She peels away a tiny sticker on the egg's underside and tips her head so the small print is visible in the bottom part of her bifocals. The price is there — £20 and the name of the shop — Portsoy Marble.

Is the egg made of marble? But surely marble comes from Italy, not Scotland. Would they import ornaments to sell along with the clan maps and tartan tea cosies? And if the egg is made from local rock, what kind of rock is it? She should have asked the shopkeeper what it was. Now she will probably never find out.

The weight and warmth of the egg bring her a feeling of comfort and she realizes now why she chose this one — its colours are the colours of Saskatchewan fields after harvest. It isn't necessary to know, to ferret out every detail of its manufacture. She will just enjoy it. She rewraps the egg in the soft paper with the holder — the holder which looks like a big wedding ring.

Ardath pulls a map from the glove box and spreads it out over the steering wheel. She decides to go on to Craigellachie. If it's bigger than its namesake in British Columbia, there may be a hotel where she can spend the night. As she refolds the map she hears a bird singing in one of the spruce trees. It sounds familiar but she can't place it until she sees a male robin on one of the lower boughs. Its markings are the same but it is about half the size of the robins at home. Song ended, the bird takes wing and flies toward the river.

Ardath starts the car and moves forward onto the road. She checks once more in the rearview mirror and what she sees reflected there is clear and pleasing to her.

Kurt's Service

She'd like to keep going forever in the clover-scented dusk. She'd like to drive right off the map. But her car has been pulling to the left, and much as she'd like to ignore it she knows she has a low tire.

She has been driving all day, with no destination in mind, at junctions turning left or right on whim, straying farther and farther from the main highways. She is stopped on the shoulder of a narrow gravel road somewhere in southern Saskatchewan. It is nearly dark.

As long as she was moving through the August afternoon with the radio turned up full blast she could empty her mind, keep memories at bay, postpone decisions. In the ditch beside a farmer's hay field it all comes rushing in on her. Physical pain is beginning to subside, and of course there will be no bruises that others can see.

There is no spare in the trunk of her car; her husband must have removed it, though she can't imagine why. She sits on the bumper of the car, careful not to lean back into the hot bug-spattered metal of the grille. The silence is broken only by the occasional screech of crows and the buzzing of grasshoppers in the ditch. She waits for half an hour, but no vehicles come by.

She doesn't want to be stranded on a deserted road in the dark; she decides to drive on. Hoping that she's not ruining the tire, she drives slowly until she sees a faint light at the roadside ahead. Two buildings appear in her headlights — a boarded-up hotel and, hunched in its shadow, a long shed. Painted letters — KURT'S SERVICE — are barely visible over the door of the shed. The only light comes from inside the building, filtered through a square of grimy glass.

She stops the car, gets out, and walks through foot-high weeds to the door. She reaches for the handle, sure it will be locked, but the door swings open easily. Inside, the building is cavernous and diabolically hot. Fluorescent lights are mounted on the ceiling and there is only one window. At the back of the shed sits an ancient Plymouth, its hood open wide in a permanent yawn. A rotary-dial telephone sits in the middle of the cement floor with a six-foot length of cord snaking out of it, connected to nothing. To the right of the door there is a high counter with three items on it: an invoice book, a manual adding machine, and a penholder which had started life as a distributor cap. On the wall beside the counter is a calendar with a picture of a little girl holding a kitten. Rubber fan belts hang on the same nail, obscuring the month and the year and casting a shadow like a noose around the child's head.

About halfway down the left side of the building two men sit side by side on a low wooden bench. A German Shepherd lies at their feet. One man has a crew cut, a wispy black beard, and a mustache. He is thin and pale and looks to be about forty years old. The other man is the same age but he is much larger, with an enormous belly hanging over a beeper on his belt. Both wear dark green work shirts and pants.

When she moves to the counter, the men don't look up but continue to stare at the floor in silence. She clears her throat and waits for them to move, but when they don't she says, "Could I get a tire fixed?" No answer. She tries again, a bit louder. "Could I get a tire fixed?" The dog growls. The men look at each other but don't answer. She'd like to run out the door and drive into the night but her car is crippled — she needs a tire. "Can I talk to Kurt?" The men are silent, motionless. At last the fat man points to his companion. Both men rise and move in unison toward her.

She opens the door and hurries outside to her car. The dog and men are right behind her. She points to the front tire on the driver's side. "Kurt" squats to inspect the flat while the other man, whom she thinks of as "Belly," inspects her. She takes a step back out of the light.

"Yep," Kurt says at last. He holds out his hand. "Keys?" She fumbles in her purse, takes out the keys and drops them into his palm, avoiding his touch. He opens the trunk, takes out the jack and wheel wrench and starts removing the tire.

Mosquitoes swarm around her, and in seconds her bare arms are covered in bites. She goes inside the building to wait. She sits on a wire-backed stool though she knows the greasy wood will stain her white skirt. She shakes her head and smiles, remembering a time when that kind of thing was all she had to worry about. Three years ago she would never have believed she would be in this situation. She was one of those people who had no sympathy for abused wives who stayed in a marriage. "Why don't they go to a crisis center? All they need to do is call the police." At that time she thought all policemen were heroes; she thought policemen were protectors.

Behind her the door creaks open and Belly and the dog file in, followed by Kurt, who is rolling a tire ahead of him into the building. Even the tire moves in slow motion.

"Can you fix it?" She jumps down from the stool.

"Maybe," Kurt says, as he flops the tire onto the cement. Belly returns to his seat on the bench, and the German Shepherd, after a low growl in the woman's direction, goes to sit on the floor beside him.

Kurt disappears into a dark corner behind the Plymouth and emerges five minutes later, carrying a pair of hunter's orange coveralls. Laboriously he pulls the heavy garment on over his clothes and tugs the zipper inch by inch up to the collar. He fits a black cap on his head and lowers the peak down over his eyes. He seems oblivious to the heat. He removes a plastic bottle from a shelf, holds it up to the light and scrutinizes the contents, then places it on the floor. From the same shelf he takes a container of green Palmolive dish-washing liquid and a container marked Tru-Glyde. Bit by bit he pours — first Palmolive, then Tru-Glyde into the plastic bottle.

He bends and begins to turn the tire, slowly squeezing soap solution on the rubber as it rotates. Turn, squeeze, turn, squeeze, turn, squeeze — the liquid leaves a slimy trail on the gray surface. Finally a thin thread of bubbles forms on the tire behind the applicator's nozzle. Kurt takes a piece of chalk from his pocket and painstakingly marks an X on the rubber at the exact center of the bubbles.

The eyes of the German Shepherd and the eyes of the man with the mammoth belly drill into the woman's back. She can feel Kurt watching her from under the peaked cap. Kurt slowly places the tire on the changer, slowly pries the tire off the rim, very very carefully applies a patch, and slowly fits the tire back on the rim. An hour from the time he begins, he rolls the tire across the floor and leans it against the base of the counter. He says nothing.

"What do I owe you?" the woman asks.

Kurt considers the question. "Six dollars."

There is a single bill in the woman's wallet — a fifty. She lays it on the counter. Kurt stares at the money for several minutes, then raises his eyes to hers. "Can't change it," he says.

She stuffs the fifty back in her purse and takes out her chequebook. As Kurt folds the cheque exactly in half, tucks it into the pocket of his coveralls, then buttons the pocket, she is struck by the thought that now he knows her name and address and he will be able to track her down. She shakes her head. There is nothing to worry about — she is not going home. No matter what her husband promises, this time she is not going back. She is never going home again.

Kurt rolls the tire out the door into the darkness. The trio of spectators follows him outside. It is at least twenty degrees cooler than it was in the building. In the puddle of light from the dirty window they watch him fit the tire onto the hub, tighten the nuts, and replace the wheel cover. Then he releases the jack, picks it up and puts it in the trunk.

One man stands on each side of the woman now and the dog is at her heels. As if in response to an unspoken command both men take a step closer to her. She can smell oil on their clothes and beer and cigarettes on their breath.

Driving off the Map

Kurt grabs her right hand and turns it palm upwards. She feels the rough touch of metal on her skin. Her heart pounds and she holds her breath; she's fled from one crisis directly into another. She stands motionless, sick with fear.

Car keys — Kurt has dropped the car keys in her hand.

"Good luck, lady," he says, walking toward the garage. The dog and Belly follow him.

She backs carefully onto the gravel road, and when she stops to shift into Drive she looks back at the men standing in the doorway. Kurt slowly lifts his hand in a hint of a wave.

Sweet-clover perfume flows through the wide open car window, and the summer air is soft on her skin. It is a fine night for travelling. She is going to drive until dawn.

Ice Road

Linton Ice Crossing. Load Limit 20,000 Lbs. Maximum Speed 50 Km/h. WARNING: Posted Load Limit Applies to Ice Road Only. All Other Ice Untested.

Judith sits in her car, reading the sign. She's never driven over the ice. She travels this road to the city in the summertime; at this spot a ferry transports cars across the lake. In winter she takes an alternate route, which is a hundred kilometres longer, to Saskatoon. On this February morning, impulse has brought her to the shores of Linton Lake. Most people in Palliser use the ice road — a narrow track, scraped clean by a Highways Department plow — a road which snakes three kilometres across the frozen lake. Judith has heard stories about cracks in the ice, about spots where the ice is thin because of gas bubbles below the surface. She's heard about narrow escapes and drownings. She is afraid.

Judith is not the kind of woman who takes chances. She has spun a cocoon of security around herself. She is single, forty-two years old, lives alone in a small house she inherited from her mother, has been a teller in the Palliser Bank ever since she left high school. She reads mysteries from the local library, plays bingo every Tuesday night, and attends the United Church every Sunday morning.

The townspeople, when they think of her at all, think of her as "good old Judith" who has memorized everyone's bank account number and makes polite inquiries about your family when she cashes your cheque. Each year she donates two pies to the Sports Day, an ice-cream pail of coleslaw to the Fowl Supper, and serves as cashier at the library's rummage sale. She is a reliable baby-sitter, Meals-on-Wheels driver, and wardrobe mistress for the Palliser Players.

Judith lives a moderate lifestyle — eats a balanced diet, takes vitamin supplements, exercises regularly, doesn't smoke or drink. Judith has a lump in her right breast.

Before her lies the snow-covered ice. Like the tracing of pencil on a white canvas, the plowed track zig-zags to the horizon. The road is five metres wide, bordered on either side by a few orange pylons to mark the route. A west wind picks up loose snow and whirls it endlessly over the surface. The landscape is as it was hundreds, thousands of years ago — the ice, the hills on the opposite shore, the leaden sky.

Judith shifts into Drive, moves slowly down the slope, over a bump, and onto the ice. She had expected it to be slippery, but beneath her tires the surface feels solid, almost like an extension of the paved road. Keeping carefully to the center of the cleared path, she drives on until land recedes in the rearview mirror. She's already travelled so far that if her car sank she wouldn't be able to get back to shore; weighed down by heavy coat and boots, she wouldn't be able to move in the frigid water, even if by some miracle she could escape from the car.

Visibility is poor out in the open. Wind, born in the Rockies and grown fierce in its sweep across the prairie, drives the snow before it; it howls past her windows and rocks her small car. Judith switches her headlights to Bright, then back to Dim. She can see only a short distance. It seems that the pylons are farther apart now, but perhaps it is only that she is driving slower.

Judith has a doctor's appointment in Saskatoon. There is no doctor in her town now and no hospital. She is glad her mother didn't live to see the closing of Palliser Union. Hannah was chief cook there for thirty-five years; she regarded the kitchen as her own. And Ward Two, where she died, was as familiar as her own bedroom. The pain of the cancer that killed her would have been unbearable if she'd been forced to spend her last months in a city hospital, far from her friends and daughter. Hannah said it felt as though thousands of worms were crawling deep inside her bones. Near the end Judith spent every night on a cot in her mother's room. In spite of the morphine she was given, Hannah suffered excruciating pain and often cried out in her sleep. On those sleepless nights when Judith prayed for her mother's suffering to end, she decided that if she ever found herself in the same situation she wouldn't wait patiently to die. Judith will refuse to be a partner in death's French minuet — advance, retreat — advance, retreat. The never-ending swings between hope and despair. Until at last death decides the dance is over. Judith will take charge of her own destiny.

Driving off the Map

She has been on the ice a long time; she should have reached the other side by now. But she can't see the hills that rise from the shoreline. Judith has heard that there are gas wells somewhere on the north side of the lake; in those spots the ice is only a few inches thick. She stops, decides to go back, but when she looks behind her, the other shoreline is invisible too. Snow needles strike the windows; they seem to come from every direction simultaneously. In minutes the snowstorm becomes a full-fledged blizzard. There is nowhere to go.

Judith turns the engine off. Immediately the air inside the car is chilled. Three-quarters of a tank of gas left, but it's impossible to know how long the storm will last. She won't start the engine and turn on the heater until the cold becomes unbearable.

Beneath Judith's feet, separated only by a thin skin of metal, is the ice. How deep? Two metres? One? A few centimetres? And below the silvery ice — water. Water churning its way to the lake bed far, far below. Black water lashing reeds, jagged rocks and big-jawed pike. Water cold as the glaciers that formed this landscape eons ago.

Judith shivers. She is conscious of the small lump on the underside of her right breast. Yesterday she went to the library, not for her usual mystery novel, but for books about breast cancer. A great many of the case histories ended with a statement of the patient's death. No matter what the doctor finds today, Judith's life will never be the same. If she has cancer, she will be plunged into the world of treatment — surgery, radiation, chemotherapy. If her lump is a simple cyst or benign tumour, she will take that as a sign that she should make changes in her life.

Forty-two isn't old; she can do the things she's always wanted to — travel, take some university courses, make new friends — maybe even find a man to share her life. Enough of letting life pass her by; now she'll be willing to take risks to get what she wants. She'll sell her house in Palliser, even though she may only get two or three thousand for it; no one wants to live in a dying town. Then she'll move to Saskatoon. Her manager will recommend her for a position in one of the bank's city branches. She can't imagine why she hasn't made the move years ago.

After an hour the wind begins to let up. Snow continues to fall, but gently now in large, fluffy flakes. Faint blobs on the horizon become the rounded hills of the shoreline. Judith realizes that snow has sifted over the plowed track and that the wind has carried the pylons away. She has strayed onto untested ice. But she sees also that she is much closer to shore than she expected. She turns on the ignition and tries once – twice – three times to start the engine. At last, it comes alive. She drives toward land.

Sun breaks through the clouds with the brilliance that often follows a winter storm, and the air is calm in the aftermath of the wind's fury. Snow is sculpted into peaks like meringue with sunlit sequins sprinkled on top. An owl flies over the lake, flapping once, then gliding, drifting in a slow arc to the horizon.

Judith's car hums over the surface; warm air whooshes from the heater vents and the radio emits the soft strains of a Brahms symphony. Then there is another sound. A deep rumble that builds and builds to a sustained moan, then an explosion like the crack of a rifle. But it is not a gunshot. It is not a sound made by man. It is the ice.

John and Mac

"Is Mac in St. Paul's or University, Dad? Dad?"

John Coleman started from his daydream. The heat in the truck cab and the hum of the engine had almost lulled him to sleep.

"Yeah. St. Paul's."

"I can drop you off there first, and after I get the hydraulic pump I'll come back and pick you up."

"Good enough." He didn't let on to Murray that he was hoping he'd come into the hospital with him. John hated hospitals, could count on the fingers of one hand the times he'd been inside one — when each of his kids was born, when Murray had pneumonia, and the time Marge got her appendix out. And that was in Palliser, not in a city hospital.

But he had to go this time. He and Mac McAllister went back a long way. John thought McAllister was the best man that ever shit over the heel of a boot. The doctors had figured at first that Mac would just be in a week or so and then he could come home to Palliser. But it had been close to a month now and still no word of him getting out. His wife, Norma, had come up to stay with her cousin to be close to the hospital.

"You know, Dad, the Andersons were up to see Mac last week. Arnie says he's in pretty rough shape."

"Mac's as tough as shoe leather. He'll likely be out any day now."

"I don't know. I guess he's a lot sicker than we thought."

"Aw, Arnie Anderson always gets everything ass backwards." He stubbed his cigarette into the ashtray. "Remember the time he went around telling everybody half of Denwald burned down and all it was was that old chicken coopa Jake Martin's. And the fire brigade had set it afire on purpose so's they could practice."

"Well, everybody says ..."

"They're giving Mac some kinda treatments. Norma told me that herself. The doctors sure as hell wouldn't be doin' that unless they figured he's got a good chance." John turned on the radio and punched the buttons until he got a song called "Old Corrals and Sagebrush." Then he turned up the volume.

Looking out at the wheat fields beside the highway, John thought about the year the old Massey combine that he'd nursed along for so many years had finally defeated him. Before harvest he'd put on new belts and replaced all the worn parts, but two rounds into his first field it quit and nothing could get it going again. When the ducks moved into the durum swathes he figured he'd lose the whole crop. Then Mac pulled into the field with his John Deere and combined all night. Left his own wheat to do it, too. You don't forget something like that.

He asked at the desk how to find Mac's room. After he was in the elevator, two nurses pushed in a bed and a wheeled contraption with bottles hanging on it. Tubes from the bottles were attached to someone in the bed. John couldn't tell if it was a man or a woman lying there. He stared at the floor.

"Did you order flowers for graduation, Cindy?"

"Oh, I just can't decide between roses and carnations. I want yellow roses, but they're *so* expensive."

"Better make up your mind. The order has to be in by Wednesday."

John could hear groans from the bed and smell the stench of anesthetic. Sweat glued his shirt to his back.

In the corridor a bored voice from somewhere in the wall ordered: "Dr. Lafferty to OR; Dr. Lafferty to OR." John moved slowly down the hall, checking the numbers on the half-open doors. At last he found the right room and pushed the door open. "How're you doin', you old bugger?" It was an old joke between them. John had said it first on Mac's fiftieth birthday, while he was still forty-nine. Now, twenty years later, it was true — they were both old men.

"Not worth a shit, John." Mac's voice was weak. "Not worth a shit." He shifted a little on the bed but didn't try to sit up. Mac's face was the bluish white colour of skim milk, and he'd always been skinny, but John had never seen him like this. His body barely disturbed the taut blankets. "Whaddya doin' up here?"

"I come with Murray. He hadda come for tractor parts, so I got him to drop me off here." John sat down in an orange plastic chair and stretched his legs out. His boot clanked against a metal handle at the foot of the bed. He pulled out a pack of Exports and was about to flick a match with his thumbnail when he saw the No Smoking sign. He put the cigarettes back in his pocket and snapped it closed. "They treatin' you alright in here, Mac?" His voice sounded too loud in his own ears. He felt he should whisper the way he did when he was a little boy sitting between his grandparents at church. "Grub okay?"

"Not too bad, not too bad. Don't get hungry now, though." Mac's fingers plucked at the white blanket. "Not like in the old days. Remember the pancakes that time — at the Snakebite Lake Stampede?" He chuckled. "You ate twenty, but I beat you. Twenty-two. Damn near busted a gut doin' it though." His laugh turned to a racking cough that shook his whole body.

Must hurt like a son-of-a-bitch, John thought. "Yeah, that was '32. You got first money in the saddle bronc and I took the steer wrestlin'." He grinned. "We didn't sober up for a week."

Mac closed his eyes. John looked at the cards on the bedside table. Most of them had Get Well Soon printed over pictures of flowers. Wilted daisies drooped in a clear-glass vase, their stems coated in green slime.

Finally Mac stirred and asked in that wispy voice, "How's the crops? Crops good?"

"In the shot-blade. But they're gonna suffer if we don't get a good rain pretty soon." He snapped the wooden match in half. "Dry again this year, Mac. Could be the dirty thirties all over again."

"Hope not. Young guys now couldn't make it. Gonna go belly-up, lots of em." Mac shook his head. "In debt — all of em. In debt, up to their eyeballs."

"Price a land, and all that big machinery they gotta have. They don't patch up the old stuff like we done."

Mac nodded. "Gotta have big machinery, all gotta have ..."

The door swung open, pushed by a plump young nurse carrying a tray. "Here's a nice glass of milk, Mr. McAllister, and your laxative." When she marched to the bed, John rose and went to the window. All he could see was another wing of the hospital and a small patch of lawn, brown around the edges where the sprinklers didn't reach. He turned to see Mac taking small sips of milk — thought of the hundreds of times he'd seen that same hand raise a glass of rye or a bottle of beer.

After the door whooshed closed, John returned to his chair. "That girl's packin' more meat than Tommy Schmidt ever had in his butcher shop."

"Ain't that the truth!" Mac started coughing again. When he finally stopped, he turned his face to the wall and lay so still that John couldn't tell if he were sleeping. The room filled with the sound of Mac's laboured breathing and the fading wail of an ambulance siren.

John didn't know if he should leave or say something. But he couldn't think of anything to talk about. It was the first time he'd been stumped on what to say to Mac — after all those years of barn talk that Marge and Norma always complained about.

John stood up. "Well, I guess I'd better go. Murray might be waiting for me." He put on his Stetson. "You better get outta here pretty soon. Haven't had a decent pool game since you left. Yesterday I hadda play Percy Leyes, for chrissake." He paused at the door. "Just let me know when you're comin' and I'll get a forty of Canadian Club. Hell — I'll get two forties, we got a lotta catchin' up to do."

Mac turned to look at him. "John, will you do something for me?"

"Name it. What do you want?" It seemed like ten minutes went by before Mac spoke again.

"Turn on the TV there. It's time for *Jeopardy*. I watch it every day."

He didn't take his eyes from the screen when John left. Just echoed the "See ya, Mac" with an abstracted "See ya, John."

When John got into the truck in the parking lot, his son asked, "How's Mac?"

John yanked open the flap of his shirt pocket. "Old bastard's not gonna make it," he said, pulling a cigarette from the pack. He didn't speak again until the city was far behind them. "Musta had a lot more rain through here." He pointed to a tractor and baler in the field beside the highway. "Good hay crop."

Taking It Easy

———— ⊱ ⊰ ————

"We shoulda taken my half-ton," John Coleman says, shifting his weight from one lean hip to the other. "This little High ... Hyundie might get good gas mileage but it rides like a Model T. How much farther to this lake anyway?"

Wayne hunches over the wheel, keeps his eyes on the road. "We should be there by noon, Dad." He steers carefully around a water-filled pothole.

"Want me to drive for a while?"

"No, you just relax. You've got to take it easy."

John stares out the window at the gray sky and the jackpines that line both sides of the road as far as he can see. There must be thousands of them — scrubby trees no good for lumber — just taking up space. A few might get cut down for Christmas trees — gussied up with tinsel and ornaments for a week or two, then thrown out with the garbage, leaving a trail of brown needles behind.

"There's nothing wrong with me. I should be home hauling grain for Murray. Haven't missed a harvest since 1932. Diane can't even start the loader, so Murray'll have to get off the combine every time and go—"

"Dad, they'll manage."

"His new grain truck's got power steering. No reason I couldn't—"

"You have to take it easy. The doctor said you can't do anything that strains your heart and—"

"Yeah, yeah."

"That attack was a warning and you—"

"Aw, I don't think it was my heart at all. I more'n likely had pleurisy again. You remember how sick I was the summer Mac died. I was so weak I could hardly get up outta bed to go to the funeral."

Any gravel that was on the road has disappeared; now there is just mud — thick and dark as axle grease. Every ten miles or so there's a trapper's cabin set back in the trees. They all look deserted. The men haven't seen another vehicle since they turned off the highway, more than an hour ago.

"It's big fat guys like your Uncle George that take heart attacks. Your mother's family all runs to fat." John pulls a package of Exports from his pocket, looks over at Wayne, then lights a smoke. "I never weighed more'n a hundred and fifty-six in my whole life."

Wayne bites his lip and rolls his window down. "It's sure hard to stay in these ruts."

"I'll drive."

"No, it's okay." Wayne eases the car around a curve, frowning in concentration as he turns the wheel slowly to the right. "I hope the road's not like this all the way to Crystal Lake."

"Tell me something, Wayne. How come you're so het up about fishing all of a sudden? Never known you to fish before."

"Not since I was nine. Remember that summer I spent every day at the dugout, trying to catch minnows?" He shakes his head and chuckles. "I figured it was time to give it another try. I've got to have better luck this time."

"How'd you manage to get time off?" John gives his son a sharp glance. "I thought you were going to take your holidays in the winter. Go to Hawaii again."

"I am. But I can take a few days now. I'm not too busy at the office, so we thought that after you got out of the hospital ..."

"We?" John says. "Who's we?"

Wayne clears his throat and closes the window.

"So that's it. You and Murray and your mother too, I suppose — you all got together and cooked up this bogus trip to get me out of the way until harvest was over." John turns to stare out the window at the weed-filled ditch and the stand of jackpines.

"Well, you're right. A man who can't pull his weight's no use to anybody."

"Oh no, Dad. That's not it. We just thought ..." The car fishtails and comes to a stop. Wayne shifts into reverse, then into low, reverse, low. The car doesn't budge. "Shit," he says, thumping the steering wheel with his fist. "We're stuck."

"Shoulda taken the half-ton." John butts his cigarette and reaches for the door handle. "I'll give you a push."

Wayne leaps out of the car. "You steer, I'll push."

Driving off the Map

When his son signals that he's ready, John guns the engine. The car surges free of the mud and John drives to the top of a hill to wait.

Wayne walks up to the door on the driver's side. His jeans and pale yellow sweater are freckled with mud and his Reeboks are so heavy he can barely lift his feet off the ground. "Slide over, Dad. I'll drive."

John ducks his head to hide a grin. "What the hell happened to you?"

"I slipped. I didn't expect you to pull away so fast."

Half an hour later they catch sight of Crystal Lake. The lake is huge — so big they can't see the other shore. It's like looking out at the ocean. A small island appears miles away in the gray expanse of water. The evergreens along the shore are dotted with yellow-leaved poplars.

The words Kuzak's Resort are painted on a thin board nailed to a pine tree. An arrow points to the left.

A mile down the road they come to a clearing on the lakeshore. There is a dock, and tied to it two old aluminum boats banging together in the swell. Fish flies hover over a filleting table a few feet from the water. Four unpainted shacks are set in a jagged line between the trees.

Wayne stops the car beside the first cabin, the one with "Resort — H. Kuzak, Prop." painted on the sagging door.

"This can't be it." Wayne takes off his glasses, wire-rimmed with tinted lenses, rubs them on his shirt and puts them on again. "There must be some mistake."

"What did you expect — one a them fancy condom ... condomin ... hotels like they have in Hawaii?" He grins and opens the car door.

"I should have checked it out, Dad. I wanted to get a nice place, where you'd be comfortable." He does up his seat belt and reaches to turn on the ignition. "We'd better look for something else."

"This suits me fine." John reaches into the back seat and grabs a tackle box. "Come on, let's get this stuff unloaded." He moves quickly. "It looks like rain. Fish always bite good just before a rain."

When Wayne comes out of the office with the key for their cabin he sees his father carrying the large metal cooler, packed with food and ice.

"Let me take that."

"I got it. Just show me what shack we're in."

"Number Three. But you shouldn't be lifting that heavy—"

"It's not heavy," he says, taking shallow breaths as he starts toward the third cabin. "Just awkward."

There is only one room, furnished with iron bunk beds, a table, a couple of chairs, and a green cupboard nailed to the wall. Inside the cupboard are two saucepans, an enamel coffeepot, some rusty cutlery, and a few plates and cups. In the middle of the room sits a wood-stove, surrounded by a carpet of gray ashes, criss-crossed with mouse tracks. A cardboard box, half-full of logs, is linked to the stove by a giant cobweb.

When they have the sleeping bags, suitcases, food, and fishing gear unpacked, Wayne sets plates out on the table. "I'll boil the kettle for tea and then we can eat. Mom made chicken salad."

"Salad. We can't fish all day on rabbit food." He bangs open the cupboard doors, looks in the oven. "Where's the frying pan? I'll cook us up some bacon and eggs."

"You know you can't eat that stuff any more." Wayne spoons salad onto two plates.

"Your grandfather loved fat pork — the fatter the better. He ate it every day of his life. And he lived to be eighty-seven, remember."

The two men eat their meal in silence and then Wayne starts clearing the table. "I'll take care of the dishes, Dad, and you can have a rest."

"I didn't come all the way up here to rest." He pulls on his jacket and picks up his fishing rod. "I come up here to fish and it's already two o'clock, so come on, let's get at it."

John sits in the bow of the rented boat. Its metal sides are pocked with dents, and fish scales swirl in a pool of oily water in the bottom. John turns to watch as Wayne tugs repeatedly on the starter rope. Finally the engine sputters to life, dies, then catches again and settles into a choppy rhythm. Slapped by white-capped waves, the boat cuts through the water, racing the dark clouds boiling across the sky.

About two miles out they come to an island, bare except for a few pines and a solitary pelican.

"This looks like a good spot," John shouts. Wayne shuts off the engine and drops the anchor. They bait their hooks and start fishing. With a smooth sweep of his arm John casts his line far out into the lake. He reels in slowly and casts again. Wayne flops his rod in a backhand and the lure plops into the water fifty feet from the boat.

Half an hour later, after dozens of casts, John feels a tug on his line. Keeping the pressure steady, he reels in slowly until his fish is close enough to be scooped up in the net. It's a small pickerel, under a pound. He takes it carefully off the hook and lowers it over the side of the boat into the water.

Three times in the next hour they pull up anchor and move to a different spot. Neither of them gets a bite.

The afternoon wears on; the northeast wind blows stronger across the lake, tugs at their jackets and caps, whips their lines in the water. When the first cold raindrops stab their faces they start back for camp. In minutes the wind-driven rain is slashing in horizontal sheets and both of them are soaked through.

For five minutes the boat fights through the waves but then it stops and begins to drift backward.

"Something's wrong," Wayne shouts. "The motor's running but there's no power."

Water washes over the gunwales as the boat wallows out of control. The men can't see land anywhere now — they are suspended in a globe of dark sky and dark water. Wayne bends over the motor and opens the throttle but it makes no difference. They continue to drift.

"Let me have a look." John stands up and moves toward the stern, planting his feet wide apart to maintain his balance.

"Dad. Go back. Sit down." Wayne's words are whipped away in the wind and he is forced to move aside as his father reaches out and shuts off the motor.

"That's what I figured." John nods. "Shear pin's broke."

Wayne groans. "What are we going to do now? We're miles from anywhere and nobody'll come along in this storm."

John reaches in his pocket and pulls out a handful of screws, washers, and nails. He chooses a three-inch nail and dumps the rest of the stuff back into his pocket. "This oughta do it. See if you can find me something to pound with."

Wayne looks down at the oily water sloshing around his ankles. He shakes his head.

"Look in my tackle box."

The wet metal is slippery in Wayne's hands but at last he gets the box open and takes out a bone-handled filleting knife.

"How about this?" he asks his father.

"Just the ticket." Using the knife handle as a hammer, John pounds the shear pin out, leaving the nail in its place. When he starts the motor, the boat shudders, then begins to plow through the waves. It takes an hour to get back to camp.

By seven o'clock they have a good fire going in the old stove. The air is heavy with the smell of cigarette smoke, wet wool, and boiled coffee. A kerosene lamp throws a circle of light on the table.

Wayne taps the deck of cards. "Your play, Dad."

"I sure hope it's not raining at home." John draws the eight of clubs and throws it on the discard pile. "Murray was going to start on the durum today."

Wayne glances out the window. "It's really lashing down out there. This could keep up for days."

"First harvest I've missed in fifty-eight years. Started on the threshing crew when I was fourteen."

"I know, Dad." He picks up a card. "King of hearts, that's the one I was waiting for! Gin." Wayne takes the coffeepot from the stove and refills their cups. "It's your deal."

John shifts the deck from hand to hand. "You know, Wayne, it's a funny thing. A man never thinks he's going to get old and sick. Thinks he can keep on working forever." He sets the cards down on the table.

Wayne looks at his father. He goes to the corner of the room, takes his suitcase and sets it on the bottom bunk, pulls out sweaters and socks and tosses them on the mattress. From the bottom of the case he lifts a brown paper bag and carries it to the table. He pulls a bottle of whiskey from the bag and pours some into their coffee cups.

John taps the bottle. "Doc says I should lay off this stuff too."

"One or two won't hurt, Dad."

John takes a drink, picks up the bottle and looks at the label. "Good whiskey."

Wayne turns the bottle top in slow circles on the table. "Maybe this trip wasn't such a great idea. If you like, we can start back in the morning."

John looks into Wayne's face. "Naw, this'll likely clear off by morning. Let's try it again. Should be some big jacks out there."

"Yeah?" Wayne says, turning the lamp wick higher. "You really think so?"

"Sure, son. Bound to be, in a lake that size."

Who Are You?

⁓ ⬧ ⁓

"I wish you would sit up here with me, Dad," Betty says. "I feel like a cab driver."

Joe meets his daughter's eyes in the rearview mirror. "I want to ride with your mother. After all, it's the last time."

"Do you have to be so melodramatic? Mom's going to a nursing home, not the electric chair." Betty pulls away from the white clapboard house, drives through the village, where more than half of the houses and businesses are boarded up, and out onto the highway. The road runs straight north between stubbled fields, the wheat stalks short and dun-coloured — acres and acres of dirty scrubbing brushes pointing their bristles at the sky.

"I'm sure you will be able to take her out for a drive on nice days."

"It's gonna take me half an hour to drive up to Linton and half an hour to come home again, so I'm not gonna waste my visiting time driving round some more." He waves his hand to the right, pointing to a deserted farmyard that is surrounded by scraggly caraganas and filled with rusted-out tractors. "Peterson's place. At one time he had the best herd of Black Angus in the district. Old Ned is long gone." Joe's voice becomes strident. "We're gonna get snow any day now. How'm I gonna get up to see her if it's a bad winter and the roads are blocked? The doctor told me not to shovel any more. Have you give that any thought?"

"Dad, the Department of Highways will snowplow, they'll keep the roads open."

"She don't have to go. I'll just tell them at the lodge that we changed our minds."

Betty takes her foot off the accelerator and the car slows to a crawl. A Purolator truck pulls around them, the driver shaking his fist as he passes. "Dad, we've been over this a hundred times. I know it's difficult, but we agreed this is the best thing for Mom."

Joe pats his wife's knee. "Shipping her off to a bunch of strangers. Them nurses won't have a clue what she wants. I'm the only one can understand her. Three years I been looking after her. Now all of a sudden I'm not good enough any more."

Betty sighs. "Nobody's saying that. You've been wonderful with her, and I wish you could carry on, but she's a lot worse now. It's too much for you. You could have a heart attack. Aunt Emma told me you've been having a lot of chest pains lately."

"That woman never could mind her own business."

"Looking after Mom would be a tough job for a young person, let alone a man of seventy-nine." She picks up speed again. "It would be different if I still lived here. I could give you a hand."

"You *would* still be here if that man of yours hadn't lost his farm. Land his granddad homesteaded. Some of the best land in the township, but that wasn't enough for your husband. Oh no, he's gotta go in debt to buy another two sections, borrowing money when interest rates was the highest they ever been in this country. Not a snowball's chance in hell of paying that back with two-dollar wheat."

"Dad, it's not fair to blame Floyd. No one ever dreamt the price of wheat would fall so low. We weren't the first to lose our farm and we certainly won't be the last. Really it has worked out for the best. Now we have two paycheques coming in every month and no more worries about the bank or the drought or the grasshoppers or ..."

"Crying shame — good heavy land like that."

Betty pretends she hasn't heard. "After Mom's settled in the lodge, why don't you hop on the bus and come out to Calgary to see us and your great-granddaughter? She's beautiful, Dad. Cindy and David are so proud of her, and so are we." She laughs. "Although I still think Floyd and I are too young to be grandparents."

They roll along in silence for a mile or two and then Joe says, "I seen a picture of her."

"Who?"

"Little Parsley. You sent us a picture."

"Dad, you know perfectly well her name is Presley."

"Dirty trick to play on an innocent little baby. Giving her a name like that. He's not dead, you know."

"Who?"

"Elvis Presley. I read in the *Enquirer* where he's frying hamburgers at a McDonald's. Idaho, I think it was." He waits for Betty to challenge him on this, but when she doesn't, he says, "Cindy shoulda called the baby after your mother."

"You don't hear many kids called Gladys nowadays."

"More's the pity. Gladys is a real nice name. It was his mother's name, too."

"Whose mother?"

"Elvis Presley's mother. I seen in the *Enquirer* her name was Gladys."

As if in response to her name, Gladys reaches out to touch her husband's cheek. "Who are you?" she says.

"See, Dad, she doesn't even know you any more."

"Of course she knows me." He shrugs off her accusation. "She means 'Where are we going?' She just can't get the words out right. Like when she first took the stroke, everything was a 'churn.' Remember? You were a 'churn.' I was a 'churn.' A roast of beef was a 'churn.' A head of cauliflower ..."

"I can't stand it." Betty's voice breaks. "Mom was so intelligent and she had such a wonderful sense of humour. But it's all gone. Everything. There's not a glimmer of her left. She doesn't even know she has a great-granddaughter. My own mother doesn't even know me. She doesn't know you."

"Course she knows who we are. Don't you, Gladys?" Joe tucks a strand of her hair behind his wife's ear. "I understand everything she says. I'm the one to look after her — not a bunch of strangers who don't know her from Adam's off ox."

"Dad, the nurses are trained to care for people like Mom. That's their job. Don't worry, she'll be fine."

"She won't know a soul there." Joe shakes his head. "She'll hate it. We're just gonna have to turn around and take her home again."

"No, we are not. Mom will adjust if you give her time. It's the best place for her. Nurses on duty twenty-four hours a day and a doctor on call if there are any problems."

"If she's got to go someplace, it should be our own town. They might open up the hospital in Palliser again, and Gladys could have a room in there."

"Oh, Dad, face facts. The hospital's closed for good; they've sold the equipment. The doctor's leaving next month. Before long, Palliser will be nothing but a ghost town."

"It could swing around. Back in the thirties times were tough, but then the drought ended and war broke out and pretty soon everybody had money again. Things could start getting better any day now."

A dozen mallards lift off from a slough beside the highway and flap into the heavy sky. Soon they will join a larger flock and migrate to a warm marsh on the coast of Mexico.

"Who's she? Who's that woman?" Gladys leans forward and points to her daughter.

"Okay, translator," Betty says. "I'm sure you'll tell me she's not really asking who I am. So what does she mean this time?"

"She's cold. That the best your heater can do?"

"Cold? How can she be cold? I'm sweating."

Joe takes off his jacket and drapes it over his wife's shoulders. "Your mother's got poor circulation. Feels the cold worse than we do. Them people at the lodge don't know that. If we was to leave her there, she'd be cold all the time."

"She won't be cold. Stop worrying."

"Al Anderson's sister's been in the lodge five years. He says the food's awful. Gladys likely won't eat a thing in there. She's used to my cooking."

"Bacon and eggs and Kraft Dinner?"

"That's what she likes. Isn't it, Gladys?"

Gladys makes a sudden lunge for the door handle. "Where's that goddamn dog?"

"Take it easy." Joe settles her back into the seat. "There's no dog. Just take it easy."

Betty slows the car. "Is she okay? Do you want me to stop?"

"No, she's fine. She got a little excited, that's all."

"She gave me a scare. I didn't think she could move so fast. And Mother swore – I couldn't believe my ears."

"She don't mean it. She uses words now she never used before. Sometimes words I didn't even think she knew." He clears his throat. "She knows we're taking her to the lodge and she don't want to go. That's what got her all wound up. Let's turn around and go home."

"We are not going home. I took two days off work to help you get Mom moved in. This was all arranged months ago; you agreed that Mother would go in as soon as there was an opening. Now there is an opening and if she doesn't take it, she'll go back to the bottom of the waiting list. It could be years before we get another chance."

"Oh no, it won't take long. As soon as one of the old geezers dies, there's an opening. And they keel over like flies in that place – there's nothing to live for."

"Dad, I know what you're trying to do; you're trying to make me feel guilty. But it won't work. We're going to Linton and Mother's going into the lodge."

Gladys is slumped in a corner of the seat, weaving her gnarled fingers together as though she is fashioning willow branches into some useful object — a basket or a wreath. Joe takes her hands in his and they continue the trip in silence.

Linton Lodge is a twenty-bed facility, geared to the needs of level three and four patients. The building is a low cream-coloured stucco structure with apple green trim on the windows and doors. Tall spruces border the grounds, and a few feet from the front entrance squats a glassed-in gazebo where on summer days the lodge residents can sit, protected from the prairie winds that have been part of their lives for seventy, eighty, or ninety years.

Inside, a nurse greets Betty and her parents and asks them to wait in the lounge while she gets Gladys's room ready. Betty gives her the suitcases filled with Gladys's belongings and, in exchange, the nurse hands her a four-page form to be filled out and signed.

"I'm sure we gave them all this information when we applied," Betty says when the three of them are seated in orange vinyl chairs in the lounge. "What's Mom's Health Services number?"

Joe pulls a plastic card from his wallet and hands it to Betty without a word. Ten minutes later Betty places the completed form on the counter of the nursing station. A harried clerk, telephone pressed to her ear, nods her thanks.

There are no magazines or books, so Betty has nothing to do but take stock of the room. Prominently displayed on the longest wall is a large bulletin board with red and yellow felt letters: "Today Is Friday, October 18th." Just as well Mother doesn't know that, she thinks. Gladys was superstitious about starting any project on that day. If Joe planned to begin seeding or harvesting on a Friday Gladys always insisted that he make one round on Thursday evening — just to be on the safe side. Under the sign, a nearly bald woman, wearing a Blue Jays tee-shirt, sits motionless at a table where the pieces of a jigsaw puzzle are spread out before her. Five wheelchairs are arranged in a semi-circle in front of a picture window, affording the occupants an unobstructed view of the parking lot. Three men are watching the Oprah Winfrey show on television. The sound is turned so low it is doubtful they can hear a word, but their eyes never leave the screen. A very tall woman, who is much younger than the others, probably in her forties, circles the room constantly. She peers intently into every face, in an endless search for something or someone she has lost. Beside Betty's chair there is a four-foot aquarium filled with plants and tropical fish. The streams of bubbles rising from the filter and the swaying movement of the fish have a hypnotic effect.

"I should never have let you talk me into this," Joe says, his words bouncing off the walls and tiled floors. "Three years I been looking after her. Ever since she took the stroke. I can take care of her better than anybody — you included. Not that I ever heard you offering to try."

"Well, I can tell you one thing, if I *was* looking after her she wouldn't look like a ... like a bag lady. Look at her. She hasn't had a haircut in months. Her skin is so dry it's flaking. There's stains all over her sweatsuit. Mom, who was always dressed to the nines, not a hair out of place. Going off to the Ladies Aid meetings in a suit, high-heeled shoes, and white gloves. How do you think she'd feel if she knew that today she's wearing one red sock and one green one?"

"Gladys wouldn't give a good goddam. Her feet are warm; that's all she cares about now. She ain't like she was when you were a kid, and she's never gonna be like that again. But she's still my wife and I know what's best for her, and it's sure as hell not sitting around here with a bunch of old fogeys waiting to die." Joe gasps for breath and presses his hand to his chest.

Betty rushes to his side. "Dad, are you okay?"

"Yah, yah, sit down."

"I'm sorry, Dad. I know you're doing your best."

Gladys stands up and peers into Joe's eyes. "Who are you?"

"I'm okay, Gladys. I'm okay." The colour returns to his face and he begins to breathe normally.

When they are all seated again, Betty says, "It's been too much for you, Dad. You're exhausted. This will work out fine, you'll see. You can come up and visit her whenever you like — every day at first, if you want to. But you'll be able to get your rest at night. You can go down to the drop-in center, play pool, visit your old friends. Mother wouldn't want you to wear yourself out for her. Remember how she always worried about your health. She'd want you to take care of yourself."

"I never thought about it like that before."

"You know it's what Mom would want."

"I have been feeling kinda wore out lately. Some days I can't get all the housework done. That part don't matter, but I'd hate to think maybe I'm not doing right by Gladys. Do you really figure she'd be better off in here?"

"I'm just asking you to try it for a few months. See how it goes."

"We been together fifty-six years. I'm gonna miss her something fierce."

"I know, Dad."

"You really think she'll be okay in here?"

"I really do."

"I spose we can give it a try. But if she hates it — if she don't settle in, I'm taking her back home."

"Let's cross that bridge when we come to it. What's keeping that nurse? She must have decided to wallpaper the room and hang new curtains."

Driving off the Map

Gladys stands up and turns toward the television watchers. She points to the man in the middle and asks in her loud clear soprano, "Who's that old prick with the big nose?"

Betty glances anxiously around the room, but none of the residents show any sign that they have heard the question or understood it. Joe coaxes his wife back into her chair.

Betty whispers to her father, "You know, Dad, the man *does* have a really big nose."

"Gigantic!"

"Humungous!"

Joe slaps his knee. "He could smoke a cigarette in a rain storm."

When the nurse enters, Joe, Betty, and Gladys are all laughing — laughing together, as they haven't laughed in years.

"Who's telling jokes in here?" the nurse asks with professional cheeriness.

"Gladys," Joe says, "is callin' 'em like she sees 'em."

"My mother," Betty says, pulling her mother into a tight hug, "has a delightful sense of humour."